A DADDY
FOR DILLON

STELLA BAGWELL

❤HARLEQUIN®SPECIAL EDITION®

Recycling programs
for this product may
not exist in your area.

ISBN-13: 978-0-373-65742-1

A DADDY FOR DILLON

Printed in U.S.A.

STELLA BAGWELL

has written more than seventy novels for Harlequin Books. She credits her loyal readers and hopes her stories have brightened their lives in some small way.

A cowgirl through and through, she loves to watch old Westerns, and has recently learned how to rope a steer. Her days begin and end helping her husband care for a beloved herd of horses on their little ranch located on the south Texas coast. When she's not ropin' and ridin', you'll find her at her desk, creating her next tale of love.

The couple have a son, who is a high school math teacher and athletic coach. Stella loves to hear from readers and invites them to contact her at stellabagwell@gmail.com.

To my readers, thank you so much
for inspiring me to tell another story
and for making my job so very worthwhile.

"You don't have children, do you?"

Her question stung him, even though it shouldn't have. Over the years Laramie had tried to picture himself as a father. But that was like imagining a ditch digger becoming a heart surgeon. It was possible. People could always learn, but along the way they were bound to make mistakes. And in his opinion a child's rearing was too important for mistakes.

"No. But I was a little boy once. That sorta qualifies me to understand Dillon's way of thinking."

Her dark eyes were making a slow sweep of him. He felt ridiculously exposed. Maybe she could see he wasn't comfortable with the idea of having a woman in his life and children looking to him for guidance. Maybe she could see that a bucking bronc or a raging bull didn't scare him in the least, but the word *love* or *marriage* terrified him.

Dear Reader,

I first met Leyla Chee in *His Medicine Woman* when she was giving birth to her son in the backseat of Johnny Chino's truck. At that time, the only thing I knew about her was that she was alone and struggling to survive. A few books later, the memory of her quiet strength remained with me and I realized she deserved to find love in her life, a home and family of her own. But what sort of man would be special enough to give her those things and also be a daddy to her son?

Laramie Jones has always been content to remain in the background. For years he's lived among a big family, but never truly belonged to one. He isn't planning to become a husband or father, but love has a way of changing a man's thinking.

Every person has their own definition of what they call home. But I think we can all agree that home is not a place, it's a sense of belonging and feeling loved. I hope you enjoy reading how Leyla learns exactly what she and Dillon need the most.

God bless the trails you ride,

Stella

Chapter One

The Chaparral ranch house was shrouded in darkness as Laramie Jones entered an atrium that also served as a back porch. The long room filled with plants and cushioned lawn chairs was faintly illuminated by a row of outside footlights, but he hardly needed a light to show him the way to the kitchen door. He knew the path by heart. This New Mexico ranch had been his home for nearly eighteen years, and for the past year he'd been residing right here in the Cantrell's family home.

About to reach for the doorknob, he instinctively jumped back when the wood and glass panel burst open and a tiny person crashed directly into his shins.

"Whoa!" Reaching down, Laramie attempted to snatch a hold on the darting child.

"Dillon! Come to me. Right now!"

The female voice was soft but firm, and Laramie quickly looked around to see a very young woman standing in the open doorway. As he stared, trying to figure out who she might be, the wayward boy scampered to her side and latched a death grip around her leg.

"I'm sorry," she said quickly. "My son doesn't normally run from me. I hope he didn't hurt you."

Her son! The boy appeared to be about three. From this limited view, she hardly looked old enough to be his mother. The light shining through the entryway silhouetted her petite figure and created a flame-colored halo around black hair that was pulled sleekly back from her face. Although her features were in shadow, he could see the faint shape of broad lips and a pair of very dark eyes. Neither of which were smiling.

"Don't worry," he assured her. "The little guy couldn't hurt me if he tried." Moving forward, he extended a hand toward her. "I'm Laramie Jones, the Chaparral foreman." She took his hand and he was immediately struck by how small and soft it felt against his. *Was this woman a guest of the ranch?* Frankie, the mistress of the ranch, was still away in Texas visiting her sons and their families, so she couldn't be a guest of hers, he decided. Perhaps she was connected to Reena Crow, the ranch house cook. This young woman was clearly Native American, as was Reena. The two might be related.

Her next words answered his questions.

"I know," she said. "I was expecting you. I'm Leyla Chee. I have your dinner ready."

She dropped her hand and quickly started back into the house with the boy in tow. Laramie stared after the two of them. This was the new cook? *She* had taken Reena's place? A few days ago, Quint had mentioned the regular cook would be heading over to Apache Wells to replace his grandfather Abe's cook, who'd had the misfortune to break his leg. But Laramie hadn't dwelled on the matter.

Who prepared his meals was the least of his concerns. Especially these days, when everything seemed to be going wrong on the ranch. Still, he'd hardly expected a young mother to be taking over the job. And where was Leyla's husband? Had he moved into the house with her?

As Laramie followed her into the house, Leyla didn't give him the opportunity to ask those questions. She and the boy quickly moved ahead of him, then passed through the kitchen doorway and out of sight. With a puzzled shake of his head, Laramie turned the opposite direction and headed upstairs to his bedroom.

Ten minutes later he returned to the kitchen, his dark hair damp from a shower, his dirty jeans and shirt replaced with clean ones.

The new cook was standing, her head slightly bent to one side as she adjusted a burner on the huge gas range. She was dressed in black jeans and a white blouse with the sleeves rolled up on her forearms. Her black hair, which must have been extremely long, was coiled into a braided knot and fastened to the crown of her head.

Immediately upon hearing his footsteps, she turned to face him and Laramie was once again struck by the youthful appearance of her face. Beneath the glow of florescent lighting, he could see her skin was a beautiful creamy tan, her lips pink, her eyes a shade just shy of black. High, rounded cheekbones were flushed with a deep rosy color and he wondered if that was a result of working over the heat of the stove or of seeing him.

Hell, Laramie, why should you make this young girl blush? She couldn't be that shy around men. She has a child.

"In the dining room," she said, pointing to an open doorway leading into the main part of the house. "Sassy is already finished cleaning for the evening. So I put everything in there for you."

The dining room? This young woman was treating him like he was someone special. Hell, he was just the foreman. Maybe she was confused and thought he was a part of the Cantrell family. "Uh—look, Leyla, I'm sorry you went to all that trouble. I always take my meals here in the kitchen."

As she walked toward him, he spotted from the corner of his eye the boy, who was sitting on the floor near the breakfast bar. He was a stocky child with sturdy shoulders. Brown hair, the color of powdered cocoa, fell across his forehead in thick, jagged bangs. A crayon was clutched in his little fist, and a sheet of lined paper lay flat between his outstretched legs. At the moment, though, the child was ignoring the crayon and paper and was staring at Laramie with a guarded expression.

"Reena said you are the boss man," Leyla reasoned.

It was Laramie who suddenly found himself blushing as he looked away from the boy and back at her. He'd been called "boss" before by the ranch hands but not by a lovely young woman like her. It made him feel way overrated.

"Well—in a way. Quint Cantrell and his mother and sister own this ranch. I only manage it for them."

"Then you are the boss. And Reena told me to serve your meals in the dining room."

Laramie shook his head, and as he did his gaze swept across her hands folded loosely in front of her. There was no wedding ring or sign of where one had been. Did that mean she was single?

Feeling like an idiot for even wondering about the woman's marital status, he said, "I don't know why Reena would have told you such a thing. I never eat in there. That's for the Cantrell family and their guests."

The color of Leyla's cheeks turned an even deeper red as she bit down on her bottom lip and glanced at her son. "I'm not sure why she told me that. Maybe I misunderstood her. Or she might have thought Dillon would bother you here in the kitchen."

"The child won't bother me," he assured her. "I like kids."

Even though it was hard to read the expressions in her features, he could clearly see a look of relief in her eyes, almost as though she'd expected him to be difficult to deal with or even mean-natured. The idea was bothersome, to say the least.

She said, "I'm sorry there was a mix-up. I'll bring everything back here to the kitchen."

She started toward the doorway, but Laramie quickly called to her. "No. Don't go to that trouble now. It's okay. I'll eat in there for tonight."

He quickly made his way to the dining room and found the wooden table, easily capable of seating twenty diners, was set for one. Not far from the plate, two fat candles were flickering and a huge bowl of fresh cut flowers decorated the center of the table.

Laramie had eaten in this room before, when the family was present and guests had been invited for one particular reason or another. To be taking a meal here alone, as though he was the patriarch of the place, felt ridiculous to him. But he'd endure it for one night to save Leyla unnecessary work.

He'd just sat and started filling his plate from an assortment of covered dishes when the cell phone attached to his belt broke the silence.

Pulling the instrument from its holder, Laramie saw the caller was Quint Cantrell. The owner of the Chaparral ranch had been Laramie's friend for many years and they worked together more as brothers than owner and foreman.

"What's up, Quint?"

"Believe it or not I'm on my way to the grocery store. Maura's craving peanut butter and the boys cleaned out the last jar this morning. Like a good husband I offered to go get some for her."

Quint had been married for a few years now to a beautiful red-haired nurse. They had two young sons, Riley and Clancy, who would no doubt grow up to be ranchers themselves. Now Maura was pregnant again with a third child who would be born in late summer. His friend had a perfect, loving family. Something that Laramie had never experienced.

"You spoil that woman of yours rotten," Laramie joked.

"Aww, she treats me like a prince, so what's a man to do?"

Laramie could have told Quint he was asking that question to the wrong man. His experience with women was the short, uncomplicated kind. Unless four dates in one month counted as long term, then he'd never had a lengthy relationship with a woman.

"I'd say you should do exactly what you're doing."

"Smart man," Quint replied with a chuckle. "So what happened at the ranch today? Nothing major, I hope."

Leaning back in the chair, Laramie swiped a hand through his damp hair. "Not today, thank God. In fact, we found those three missing horses. They were at the back of the property. Not far from Tyler Pickens's boundary fence."

"How in hell did they get back there? Did you find any downed fences between you and Pickens's land?"

"No. But we've not yet had time to check every fence line."

"That would take days," Quint said. After a long, thoughtful pause he added, "And you don't have the manpower to waste on that right now. You're going to need all hands for spring roundup. Since the horses were found, let it be for now."

For the past few months, the Chaparral had been experiencing incidents that couldn't be explained. Like sick cattle, missing horses and perfectly good machinery suddenly going on the blink. Both Laramie and Quint wanted to believe the occurrences were just a string of bad luck, but as the problems grew, that idea was harder and harder for the men to accept.

"Right. Branding is more important. And there isn't a man on the ranch who isn't excited about roundup. I'd probably have a mutiny if I sent a few off on fence line detail."

"Worse than a mutiny," Quint agreed. After a moment's pause, he went on, "Actually, the main reason I'm calling is to see if Leyla arrived."

"I met her a few minutes ago. I'd forgotten you'd mentioned the change in cooks. I didn't remember it was going to take place this soon."

"Hell, Grandfather was having a fit to get Reena out to his place. I'm not sure she was wild about the move, but she doesn't want the old man getting stirred up."

"Abe is a tough old codger when he doesn't get his way."

"You're right. I have enough on my plate without that. Especially with Maura pregnant again. You know, Laramie, I want this baby so much—just as much as our other two boys. But I worry about Maura because I can't slow her down. She's forty but acts like she's twenty." He suddenly paused, then let out an apologetic chuckle. "I'm sorry, Laramie. That's enough about me. I should be asking if Leyla can cook. If not I'll have to find someone else to suit you."

"Can't tell you that yet. I just sat down to eat when you called."

"Damn, it's late," Quint cursed. "You should have quit work two hours ago."

"Just like you keep sane hours?"

Quint let out a snort. "Maura tries to keep me on schedule. Sometimes I make it to the house by dark at least three evenings a week."

"I'm not hurting myself." And he would make it clear to Leyla that there was no need for her to hang around to serve his meals if he came in late at night.

Quint suddenly cleared his throat. "I don't ask much of you, do I?"

Perplexed by his friend's question, he frowned. "You don't ask me to do anything that you wouldn't do. Why?"

"This is probably going to sound crazy, but I hope that whenever you are in the house you'll be easy on Leyla."

A frown quickly replaced Laramie's grin. "Why wouldn't I be easy? I'm not exactly a ladies' man, but I know how to be mannerly."

"Yes, you're always a gentleman. But I… Well, Maura and I would appreciate it if you'd be extra kind to her. She's gone through some rough spots in her life. It's time somebody treated her kindly."

"Oh. Does she—" concerned that she might suddenly enter the dining room and hear him, Laramie lowered his voice "—have a husband?"

"No. The only family we know of her having is an aunt and Oneida is elderly and in the nursing home. My sister-in-law, Bridget, and her husband, Johnny, delivered Leyla's boy in the backseat of a vehicle a few years ago. She'd been trying to drive herself to the hospital down on the res. The road was deep with snow and she'd gotten stranded. It was fortunate they found her. Otherwise, she or the baby might not have made it."

Laramie was momentarily stunned. He couldn't imagine the young woman enduring the pain of childbirth while being stranded in a freezing, snowbound vehicle. She must have been terrified. She must have felt the whole world had deserted her.

"Damn, that's tough."

"Yeah. She told Bridget that her family was dead. But we're wondering if she might have folks somewhere and split from them for some reason."

"You mean like she might have run away?"

"Nowadays who can tell? Whatever happened, it's clear that no one is around to give her any support."

"I see," Laramie said, even though he didn't. How could a woman like her be so alone? "And I promise not to give her a hard time."

"Good. Now eat your supper and I'll talk to you tomorrow."

Quint quickly ended the call, and after Laramie had put his phone away, he focused his attention on the food on his plate. But as he ate the roast beef and vegetables, his thoughts were spinning with Leyla and her young son.

Even if she'd separated herself from her parents, there was a man somewhere who'd gotten her pregnant. Why wasn't he around? The boy needed a father. Just like Laramie had needed a father all those years ago, he thought.

But you had a father. Diego Jaime might not have planted the seed in your mother's womb, but he'd cared for you, loved you just as though he'd been your father. You don't have a right to feel cheated or sorry for yourself, Laramie.

He was trying to squash the little voice going off in his head when he heard footsteps entering the dining room.

Looking up, he watched Leyla walking toward him, a pitcher of iced tea in her hand.

"Would you like your glass refilled?" she asked.

He placed the glass near the edge of the table to make it easier for her to reach. Still, she drew near enough for him to catch a whiff of her musky scent.

As she poured the tea, he said, "The food is delicious. You're a very good cook."

"Thank you."

"I didn't realize Reena was going to be leaving so soon. You must have gotten here after breakfast this morning."

Nodding, she said, "Mr. Cantrell was eager for her to get to Apache Wells. Jim, his cook, has a broken leg. They're not certain how many weeks it will require a cast. So she'll be there. I'll be here."

"Yes. Quint told me."

Her lips pressed slightly together and then she looked away from him to a shadowy spot across the room. "I forgot. You're the boss. You would know those things."

He wanted to reiterate to her that he wasn't the boss, especially not hers, but he kept the words to himself. She needed time to get used to him and her new surroundings without him correcting her on every little issue.

"Have you ever lived on a ranch?" he asked.

Her gaze was quick to return to his face. "No. Why do you ask that?"

Laramie wasn't exactly sure why the question had slipped out of him. Except that she seemed a little lost. And after hearing what Quint had said about her, he didn't want her feeling that way.

"Just curious. It's a heck of a lot different from living in town."

"I haven't lived near a town in a long time. Before I came here I lived in the mountains on the res. Alone," she added, her chin jutting slightly forward, as though he needed to understand that she could take care of herself.

Her spark of independence surprised him. It also caught his admiration. "That's good. I mean, you should get along fine here, then."

Leyla gave him a faint nod, then turned and left the room. Once she reached the kitchen, she set the iced tea in the refrigerator, then leaned weakly against the cabinet counter.

Reena had told her that Laramie was a nice man and that she wouldn't have any problems with him. But the woman hadn't warned her that he was young and so good-looking. No. Good-looking wasn't exactly the right description for the ranch manager, she thought. With his tall, lanky frame and dark shaggy hair, he was more sexy than handsome.

Not since Dillon's daddy had she looked so closely at a man. She'd even noticed Laramie Jones's eyes. They were an unusual mixture of blue and brown with lights and shadows waltzing sensually in their depths.

Oh, my, this was the man she would be cooking for. She was going to have to be very careful around him. Careful not to let herself look or dream.

Reena had said he was single and stayed in this big fancy house. His room was upstairs. The maid, Sassy, had shown her which one just in case she should ever need to alert him in the night for an emergency. Thankfully, the young red-haired maid would be taking care of his room and laundry.

"Mommy, Mommy."

The tug on her leg had her glancing down at her nearly three-year-old son. He was holding a piece of paper that she'd cut from his coloring book. The wild orange markings went from the pony in the middle of the page to the very edges.

"That's a very good job, Dillon. You made the pony orange. Can you say orange?"

The boy puckered his mouth in an O as he pondered his mother's request. "Orr-range. Orr-range."

"Good. Very good." She took his small hand and led him over to the kitchen table. "And because you colored such a pretty picture, I'm going to give you some cookies and milk. Want some?"

He nodded enthusiastically and Leyla lifted him onto one of the chairs and smacked a kiss on his cheek. Dillon was the hope and dream of her whole world. Her love for him was so great that just thinking of him brought tears to her eyes. It didn't matter that his father had been a deceitful jerk. That he'd run fast and hard as soon as he'd learned Leyla was pregnant. Having her precious son made up for being discarded, for the lonely, solitary nights and for the long hard hours she'd worked to keep a roof over their heads.

"Cookies, Mommy! Eat."

"Okay, hold your horses. I'm getting it."

She'd served the boy fig wafers and milk and was cleaning the dirty pots she'd used for cooking when she heard boot steps behind her.

Glancing over her shoulder, she saw the ranch foreman carrying his plate and glass toward her.

"Here're my dirty dishes." He placed the dishes on the counter. "The meal was delicious. Thanks."

She looked up and as her gaze connected with his, her heart beat very fast. "You don't have to praise my cooking. Just tell me when something is wrong." She turned back to the sink and began to scrub one of the pots with a copper scouring pad. "Would you like dessert and coffee? Or more tea?"

"Well, I do sorta have a sweet tooth. Whatever you have is fine and a little coffee with it would be great. If this young man will share his table with me, I'll sit over here," he told her.

Leyla glanced over, expecting to see her son jump from the table and race over to the safety of his mother's side. Instead, she was slightly amazed to see Dillon stare curiously up at the big man sitting next to him.

"Is your name William or Dillon?" Laramie asked the child.

Confused and a bit insulted by a question he considered silly, he practically shouted. "Dillon!"

"Oh. Pardon me, partner. I thought you were William."

Dillon shook his head and looked hopelessly to his mother, then back at Laramie.

Suddenly remembering the rancher was waiting for her to serve his dessert, she got busy collecting a mug of coffee and a piece of apple pie. Behind her, she could hear Laramie Jones chuckling softly.

The sound was low and smooth and pleasing like the call of a night bird on a still summer evening.

"How old are you, Dillon?" he asked her son.

As Leyla carried the food and drink to the table, Dillon held up one finger for Laramie to see.

"One. Hmm, I sure thought you were older than that."

In response Dillon held up two fingers. "That many," he said.

"Well, you sure are big for two," Laramie commented.

"Technically Dillon is right. He's two. But he'll be three in a couple of weeks," Leyla told him. She placed the pie and coffee in front of him while trying not to notice the scent of him—horses and leather, grass and sunshine all rolled together. It was a very masculine scent and one that she found far more appealing than something manufactured from a bottle.

"Oh. That's what I was guessing. About three," Laramie told her.

His comment surprised her. "You know about children, Mr. Jones?"

"Not much. But Quint has two boys and I've watched them grow up," he said, then added with a frown, "and don't call me Mr. Jones. I'm Laramie to everyone."

Leyla felt herself blushing and she instinctively backed away from him. "Okay—Laramie."

"And another thing," he said. "Most days I work well after dark. There's no need for you to hang around in the kitchen until I come in. Just leave something in the warming drawer on the stove."

For some reason his instructions hurt. It was almost like he was telling her he didn't want her or Dillon's company. But then some men didn't like the chatter of a child or a woman fussing around him. Perhaps Laramie was one of those men, she thought.

"It's my job to serve you. That's what Quint pays me for. If I don't do my job I might as well move home."

"Where is that?"

The wariness she was feeling about his question must have shown on her face because he suddenly shrugged and said, "Never mind. You don't have to tell me that."

Telling herself he was only making conversation, not digging into her past, she said, "My aunt's house is on the reservation. That's where I live."

A faint grin curled up one corner of his lips. "Then you probably feel right at home here in the mountains."

Leyla hadn't felt like she was really home in a long, long time. She'd left her home near Farmington more than three years ago when she'd been four months pregnant with Dillon. Since then she'd not talked or corresponded with her parents. And she had only talked on the phone to her sisters on rare occasions. She missed her mother, Juanita, and two sisters very much. But she'd not been that close to her older brother, Tanno, because he was more like their father, George, a lazy man who thought being born a male made him superior to all women. Leyla had often considered contacting her mother, especially since Dillon had been born, but she knew to do so would only cause her to endure more misery from George. For now she had to be content with the fact that her sisters had informed their mother about Dillon and that her grandson was healthy and happy.

"Yes. I feel comfortable here," she told him.

"Will you be living here in the house?"

She nodded. "In Reena's rooms. The drive from the reservation would take hours. And my old car wouldn't hold up."

And that was enough talking with this man, she thought, as she turned and headed back to the sink full of dirty pots. She'd already exchanged more information with him than she should have. She would only be here on the ranch for as long as it took for Jim's leg to heal and Reena to resume her position as Chaparral cook.

After that, she would return to the reservation and try to gather enough funds to start nursing school. So while she was here on this huge, fancy ranch, she would keep her mind on her own business and never forget her plans for the future. A future that only included her and Dillon.

It certainly didn't include dreams of a tall, shaggy-haired cowboy with a crooked grin and fascinating blue and brown eyes.

The mere thought of the ranch manager had her peeping over her shoulder, and what she saw virtually stunned her.

Dillon, her shy little boy who rarely ever took to strangers, especially male strangers, was now sitting in Laramie's lap as though he'd just found his daddy.

"Dillon!" she said with a shocked gasp. "What are you doing?"

"We're eating," Laramie explained with a grin. "You see, me and your son have just agreed we're going to be saddle pals. And saddle pals always share their food."

Leyla stared in wonder. The man had come in dirty and tired. No doubt he'd put in a very long day. Yet he was patient enough to take time out of his evening to show her son a bit of attention and kindness. The idea stung her eyes with tears and she swiftly turned back to her dishwashing before the rancher could see he was melting her heart.

Oh, why couldn't she have met this man before her life had gotten complicated and she'd become a single mother?

She snuck a glance through the mist of her tears at Dillon sitting on Laramie's knee. He was the sort of man her son needed for a daddy. But she'd be crazy to let that sort of thought grow. A man like him was out of her reach. Or was he?

Chapter Two

The next day Laramie and Russ Hollister, the resident veterinarian for the Chaparral, drove into Ruidoso to look over several new high-protein grains being offered at a local feed store. With Laramie considering cost and storage of the grains and Russ the nutrition, the two men were able to come up with a blend that would fit the ranch's feed program.

On the way home, Laramie glanced at the clock on the dashboard of the truck. "You in a hurry to get back to the ranch?" he asked the other man.

"No hurry. Laurel is at the barn if some sort of emergency comes up. She can deal with most anything."

"Yeah. I've noticed. You'd better watch out or you might lose your job to her," Laramie joked.

Russ chuckled. "I've taught her pretty well."

About two months ago Russ had married Laurel, his longtime assistant. She was also expecting their first child and Laramie had never seen a happier pair, unless it was Quint and Maura. Love, marriage and kids. Laramie had lived around those things for many years now. Yet he still felt like he was on the outside looking through the window. It was great for his friends, but he wasn't cut out for that sort of life. He was a solitary man. Just as Diego had been.

"I have some property just off the main highway," he told the vet. "If you don't mind I thought I'd stop by and check on the place. It would save me an extra trip."

"Sure. I'd like to see it," Russ told him.

Five minutes later, Laramie turned the truck onto a graveled county road. Another half mile passed as he drove through low hills covered with scrubby juniper and sage. Green grass and wildflowers splashed the red ground with vibrant color.

"There's a house," Russ commented. "Is that on your property?"

Laramie steered the truck onto a driveway and eased it down the steep graveled slope. "Believe it or not, I used to live in that house, Russ. With the man I called my father."

"Called?" Russ repeated curiously.

Laramie parked the truck in front of the little four-room house. The cream-colored stucco was freshly painted, and the wooden shingles were all in place. Ever since Diego had died and Laramie had inherited the place, he'd made a point of keeping the structure in good condition.

"Diego Jaimc wasn't my father by blood," Laramie explained. "But I was only a few days old when he took over my raising."

"Really? Where is he now? It looks like no one lives here."

"Diego died when I was a teenager—just sixteen. He didn't have a wife, so it was just me and him. He'd always told me that if something ever happened to him to go to

Lewis Cantrell. So that's what I did. I went to the Chaparral and asked the man for a job." Laramie's sigh was wistful. "For some reason I'll never understand, Lewis took me in like his own. And I'll be forever in his debt."

"Lewis was a good judge of character," Russ told him. "And I figure you've repaid him many times over."

Laramie shot him a skeptical look but didn't pursue the subject. Diego and Lewis had both played a prominent role in Laramie's life. He hated that both men were gone now, but he felt very blessed to have been part of their lives.

"I'll just walk around the house and make sure it hasn't been vandalized," he told Russ. "Just sit if you'd rather."

"I need to stretch. I'll walk with you," the other man replied.

The two men climbed out of the ranch truck and started around the small house. The spring day was warm and the snow melt had glutted the rivers and streams to full banks. Not far from the house, the sound of rushing water mingled with the singing birds. Further off, a cow bawled to its calf. The sights and sounds always brought Laramie back to his days as a young boy when he'd explored and played over these hills. Diego had always owned a few cows, sheep and horses. Not to mention the dogs and cats that had called the place home. Three-fourths of Laramie's childhood had been spent outdoors and he'd basically been a happy boy. Even if he'd not had a set of real parents.

"I didn't realize we were birds of the same feathers," Russ said as they rounded the back of the structure.

"How's that?" Laramie asked.

"I grew up with just a mother and she died when I was seventeen."

Very surprised by Russ's admission, Laramie glanced over at the other man. "What about your father?"

"My parents divorced. After that he was a no-show."

"Hmm. At least you know who he was," Laramie mused aloud.

"So do you," Russ told him. "Your father was Diego Jaime."

Laramie's faint smile was full of fond memories. "Yeah. You're right." Diego had been a father in every sense of the word. But there were still times when he wondered what had really happened with his mother. Why she'd left her baby with a neighbor and never returned. The story had never made sense to Laramie, and he'd often wondered if the old man was only giving him the partial truth of the matter. But he'd never pressed Diego on the subject. After all the sacrifices the old man had made for him, it would have seemed very ungrateful to call him a liar. Besides, if his mother had really wanted her son in her life, then she could have returned. The fact that she'd stayed away gave Laramie at least one answer to his questions.

That afternoon, Leyla was deboning a stewed chicken when Sassy emerged from the laundry room carrying a laundry basket of just dried linen.

"Mmm. That smells good. What are you cooking?" the maid asked. She plopped the basket onto the kitchen table and walked over to where Leyla was standing in front of a long work island.

"Chicken pot pie. Do you think Laramie eats things like that?"

The tall redhead made a palms-up gesture. "No idea. That guy is hardly ever around the house when I'm here. And even when he is around, he's not exactly a talker. Believe me, I've tried."

Not a talker? Leyla had thought the man had talked very much last night, especially considering he'd only just met her and her son. This morning at breakfast he'd not said much to her, but he'd mostly been on the phone, giving orders to the men who worked under him.

Leyla looked at the maid. The woman was only twenty-four, but she seemed eons older in experience than Leyla's twenty years. She'd told Leyla that she'd worked at the Chaparral for the past eight years. It hadn't taken Leyla long to figure out that Sassy liked men but equally enjoyed being single and free.

"Oh. You were attracted to him?" Leyla asked her.

Sassy laughed as she returned to the table and plucked a sheet from the laundry basket. "Are you kidding, honey? What woman in her right mind, wouldn't be attracted to that hunk of man? But it only took me about two days to figure out he wasn't my type and I wasn't his. Although I'm not sure Laramie Jones has a type. Nobody around here has ever seen him with a woman."

Leyla found that very hard to believe. "He's a very busy man," she reasoned. "And I think his work means a lot to him."

The maid wrinkled her nose. "Well, I like a man with a work ethic. But I want him to save some of his time for me, too. You know what I mean? In my opinion, all work and no play makes a very dull boy. And speaking of boys, where's Dillon?"

"Taking a nap. He should be waking in a few minutes."

Sassy grinned. "That son of yours is so cute it almost makes me want a kid of my own. Almost," she added with a laugh.

"Have you ever been in love?" Leyla asked her curiously, then scolded herself. It wasn't like her to ask people personal things. It wasn't like her to talk much, period. But Sassy was a chatterbox and no subject seemed to be off-limits.

Another laugh bubbled past Sassy's pink lips, and Leyla

wondered what it would feel like to be so carefree and full of laughter, to think of life and men as something to be enjoyed instead of feared. Or was Sassy just putting up a front with her furtive laughter and all her talk about men? Maybe on the inside the young maid was just as lonely and needy as she was, Leyla thought.

"Oh, Leyla, I've thought I was in love at least ten or twelve times. Mostly when I was in high school. Girls are so stupid at that age." She shook out the sheet and began to fold it into a flat square. "Well, maybe I shouldn't say stupid. More like vulnerable. Me and my girlfriends believed every guy who kissed us was a hero or prince. And each of us was the only princess in his kingdom. Thank God I outgrew that mentality."

Leyla's heart went suddenly cold. "Dillon's father made all kinds of promises," she said in a low, flat voice. "And I was stupid to believe him."

Sassy covered her open mouth with her fingertips. "Oh, Leyla," she said after a moment. "I'm sorry. I was just prattling on. I wasn't talking about you."

Leyla cast her a rueful smile. "It doesn't bother me to admit I was a silly girl, too. Heath—Dillon's father—was a smooth talker. But it was all lies. I learned many things from him. Things I will never forget," she said bitterly. "A woman has to look out for herself. A man won't do it for her."

Frowning now, Sassy placed the folded sheet on the table, then walked over to the work island. "Leyla, I'm not going to ask you what happened in your past. Clearly he was a bastard anyway. I just don't believe you ought to hate all men because of him."

"I don't hate men. I just have a hard time trusting them," Leyla clarified.

Sassy groaned. "Hate. Mistrust. Either way, it tells me

you don't want a man in your life. And that's just a downright shame."

"Maybe for you," Leyla said with quiet certainty. "For me it's the right thing. At least for now, while my son is young."

With a long sigh of frustration, Sassy returned to the laundry she'd left on the table. "Okay. I'm just hoping Reena is gone for a long, long time."

Frowning, Leyla tossed a handful of chicken bones into a stainless steel bowl. "Why would you say something like that? This is Reena's home. I'm only here temporarily."

"Temporary or not. I need enough time to work on you. And before you leave, you'll be hunting yourself a husband."

"A husband!" Leyla shook her head. "Why would I need one of those?"

"Because," the maid cheerfully pointed out, "you need a daddy for Dillon."

For the first time in weeks, Laramie arrived home before dark, a feat that almost made him feel guilty. But as he parked the truck at the back of the ranch house, he reminded himself that roundup started in two days. He and every man on the place deserved a bit of rest before the week-long work marathon began.

Stepping through the yard gate, he heard Dillon's shrieks of laughter, and though he'd often heard Quint's boys loud at play, something about this child and his happy giggles caught Laramie in a way that caused him to pause and look across the yard.

Dillon and Leyla were at the gym set Frankie had purchased long ago when her first grandchild had been born. The boy was in one of the swings, while his mother was twisting and twirling him in a slow spinning ride.

"Faster, Mommy! Faster!" he urged.

"I can't go faster. Besides, Mommy doesn't want you to fall," she told him.

Laramie continued up the pathway, then stopped when he got even with mother and son. "Aww, come on, Mom, a little faster won't hurt."

Upon hearing his voice, she looked around in surprise. Laramie was instantly struck by her natural beauty. A long skirt with tiny red flowers on it swirled against her legs and molded to the curves of her hips, while her white blouse made a vivid contrast to her brown skin. Sunlight gleamed in her black hair and painted a rosy-gold hue across her cheekbones. How any man could have made a child with her and then walked away was beyond him.

"Laramie! Oh, I wasn't expecting you this early!" Quickly, she snatched Dillon from the swing and started leading the boy to the house.

The child promptly attempted to stick his heels in the ground and protest. "I wanna swing, Mommy! Let me swing!"

"Come on, Dillon. We have to go inside now so I can serve Laramie his dinner."

Laramie stepped forward. "Let me push Dillon on the swing," he said to Leyla, "while you finish what you need to do."

She looked vaguely suspicious, as though she doubted his child-caring abilities. Or she simply couldn't believe he was offering to watch her son for a few minutes. Either way put him in a bad light and that bothered the hell out of Laramie for many reasons.

"He's been out long enough," she said. "He can go with me."

He gave her a meaningful grin. "Trust me, Leyla, a boy can never be outdoors long enough."

He must have gotten his point across, because she loosened her grip on Dillon's hand and allowed him to run back to the gym set.

"How can you know that?" she asked. "You don't have children, do you?"

Her question stung him even though it shouldn't have. Over the years Laramie had tried to picture himself as a father. But that was like imagining a ditchdigger becoming a heart surgeon or a janitor evolving into a business tycoon. Of course, it was possible. People could always learn, but along the way they were bound to make mistakes. In his opinion, though, a child's rearing was too important for mistakes.

He said, "No. But I was a little boy once. That sorta qualifies me to understand Dillon's way of thinking."

Her dark eyes were making a slow sweep of him and Laramie suddenly felt ridiculously exposed. Maybe she could see he was a man who wasn't comfortable with the idea of having a woman in his life and children looking to him for guidance. Maybe she could see that a bucking bronc or a raging bull didn't scare him in the least, but the word love or marriage terrified him.

"Okay," she finally said. "He may stay. Just don't let him out of your sight. He loves to explore and will be gone in a flash if he sees something that catches his eye."

"Don't worry. I'll stick right by him."

She gave him a single nod, then turned and hurried into the house. Laramie walked over to where Dillon had climbed back into the swing.

"Hi, partner," he said to the boy.

Dillon's response was a shy little grin and a drop of his head. Warmed by the boy's acceptance, Laramie ruffled his dark hair.

"How about me and you swinging together?" Laramie suggested.

Taking Dillon's silence as an agreement, Laramie eased his tall frame onto the small wooden swing. Thankfully Frankie had spared no expense on the gym set. The sturdy quality made it capable of supporting an adult's weight also.

"Go," Dillon said, while pointing to Laramie and the swing. "Go high!"

Laramie chuckled. Apparently this wasn't Dillon's first time on a swing. "Okay. I'll go if you'll make yours go, too."

Dillon immediately began to kick his legs in an effort to put the swing in motion. Laramie reached over and gave the boy a little push to get him started.

"Yippee! I'm goin' fast 'n' high!"

"Wow! You are going fast," Laramie agreed as he carefully kept his own seat at the same gentle pace as Dillon's. "You must be a really strong young man."

Deciding it was more important to display his strength, Dillon leaped from the swing. Standing directly in front of Laramie, he held up his arms and, with a fierce grit of his teeth, attempted to make muscles. "See. I'm big. Mommy says I'm big."

Totally charmed by the little guy, Laramie leaned forward and made a show of feeling Dillon's tiny upper arms. "Your mommy is right. You're going to grow up to be a big man."

"Big. Like you."

Dillon stepped forward and patted his small hand against Laramie's knee. The child's response touched him in a way that took him by complete surprise. Whenever Quint's sons were around they were hardly shy about showing him affection. If they weren't climbing all over him, they were hugging his neck and calling him Uncle Laramie. But Riley and Clancy were very different from this little boy. Unlike the Cantrell boys, Dillon didn't have a loving daddy who was always around to protect and provide for him, to guide and support him. From what Quint had told him, he had no one but his mother. Just like he'd had no one but Diego.

Clearing an unexpected tightness from his throat, he said, "You're going to be way bigger than me, Dillon."

The boy moved closer and Laramie gently curved a hand around his shoulder. "Have you ever ridden a horse?"

His dark eyes wide with wonder, the child shook his head.

"Do you know what a horse is?"

Dillon nodded. "Orange."

With a comical frown, Laramie asked, "What?

"Orange," Dillon repeated.

"I'm not talking about a piece of fruit, Dillon. I   "

Before Laramie could finish, Dillon was grabbing his hand and urging him from the swing.

"I gotta horsey. Orange."

Very curious now, Laramie allowed the child to lead him into the house. Once they were in the kitchen, he expected the boy to turn him loose and let Leyla explain the horse matter. Instead, Dillon continued tugging until the two of them were standing in front of the refrigerator.

Several papers were attached to the appliance with colorful magnets, and when Dillon pointed to one with a horse scribbled with crayon, Laramie suddenly understood.

"Oh, I see. You have a horse the color of an orange. Hmm. That's some great work there, Dillon. Your horse must be a color that's somewhere between sorrel and chestnut."

Dillon emphatically shook his head. "Orange."

Laramie threw back his head and laughed, while somewhere behind him, Leyla said, "He's strong-minded."

He turned to see her placing a huge pie pan in front of his plate. Her movements were smooth and graceful, tempting his gaze to follow the curve of her waist and hips, the press of her blouse against her breasts. She was a beautiful and sensual girl. But still, a girl. It wouldn't be wise to let himself be attracted to her.

She's more than a girl, Laramie. She's a woman with a child. Maybe you don't want to acknowledge that because you're afraid you could let yourself get all tangled up in her.

Jerking his thoughts back to the present, he said, "It's good that your son is strong-minded. That's the way a man should be."

Turning away from the table, she motioned for Dillon to come to her. "Come along, Dillon, so that Laramie can eat his dinner."

"Me eat! Me eat, too!"

Leyla rounded the work island and took her son by the hand. "Okay. We'll go wash your hands and then you can sit at the breakfast bar. But you must be quiet and polite while Laramie is eating."

"Why can't he sit with me?" Laramie asked.

Leyla tossed him a guarded look. "I— Because this is not his home. You—"

"This is his home for as long as he's here," Laramie pointed out. "And we're partners. We're supposed to eat together. Right, Dillon?"

The boy nodded eagerly at him, then cast an uncertain look up at his mother. With a sigh of resignation, she said to Laramie. "This is not the way it should be."

He grinned at her. "How is it supposed to be, Leyla?

With you and Dillon hiding out of sight, while I sit and eat alone? That doesn't make much sense, does it?"

"I was not hired to—"

"You were hired to cook my meals. If you don't want to eat with me, that's fine. I'll accept that you don't like my company. If you and Dillon would like to eat with me, then I'd be pleased."

He watched a range of conflicting emotions pass over her face, the main one being surprise. And he suddenly realized she was trying to keep her distance because somewhere in her past she'd been made to feel unwanted and she was naturally assuming that he didn't want her around.

Finally, she said, "Since Dillon and I haven't eaten yet, I suppose it would all right."

"Good. I'll go wash up and be right back," he told her.

Minutes later, Laramie sat eating chicken pot pie and wondering if it was him or men in general that put Leyla on guard. Even though she'd agreed to sit and eat with him, she'd said little more than five words. Dillon hadn't said much more, but Laramie figured while Leyla had taken the boy to wash his hands, she'd instructed him to remain quiet. Laramie admired her for teaching the boy to have manners, especially at the dinner table, but he missed the child's spontaneous chatter.

If Dillon was his… He suddenly brought his thoughts to a screeching halt. Dillon wasn't his and he needed to remember that the child's rearing was none of his business. But that didn't mean he needed to stay completely silent.

"Dillon, do you like cats and dogs?"

"Cat. Tommy went bye-bye," the child said as he poked a bite of food into his mouth.

Laramie looked to Leyla to see her lips were pressed to a grim line. The sight made him wonder how it would be to taste those lips, to ply apart their hardness until they were full and sweet and soft against his.

"We had a cat named Tommy," she explained. "But I had to give him away because we were moving here. Dillon wasn't too happy about that. But he has to learn that giving up things is a part of life."

Laramie shook his head. "Why in the world did you think you had to give the cat away? He would have been perfectly welcome here on the ranch. We have at least fifteen or twenty barn cats running around the place. He could have joined them for a mouse dinner."

"Mouse dinner," Dillon repeated with a toothy grin at his mother. "I want some mouse dinner, too, Mommy."

Laramie couldn't keep from chuckling, while across the table Leyla's features were strained, to say the least.

"I don't expect an employer to take on my problems," she said to Laramie. "And I would never ask for favors."

One little cat? Dear God, this young woman was either very independent, or hated accepting help from anyone, he thought. Or maybe she believed she had to make sacrifices in order for people to accept her.

"Look, Leyla, I think you need to understand that around here everyone is like a big family and we try to help each other anyway that we can."

She stared at her plate and Laramie suddenly felt terrible. Not because he believed he'd sounded too rough on her, but because she seemed so utterly estranged from people.

"We will only be here for a little while," she said. "I do not intend to become a part of this family."

It was all Laramie could do to keep from slamming his fork down on the table and shouting at her. And if it hadn't been for Dillon's presence he probably would have. Which was crazy. This woman's behavior or attitude shouldn't be affecting him in any manner, but something about her made him more frustrated than he could remember being in a long time. What was it going to take, he wondered, to make her feel truly welcome and wanted here on the Chaparral?

"Well, maybe you don't, but little Dillon needs to be a part of it. Just because you want to be standoffish doesn't mean he needs to follow his mother's example."

Lifting her head she glared at him. "Dillon is my son. Not yours."

Laramie knew if he remained at the table, he was going to say something he'd regret. So he simply put his fork aside and rose to his feet.

"Thanks for the meal. I've got work to do." He gave Dillon an affectionate pat on the head, then quickly left the room.

Dillon is my son. Not yours.

Leyla had not only put him in his place, he thought, as he slowly trudged his way upstairs to his room, but she'd also made him see he was making a fool of himself. He'd allowed that little domestic scene back in the kitchen to set his mind to dreaming. But she'd jerked him awake real fast.

He wasn't a husband or a father, nor did he have any plans to be. And he should thank Miss Leyla Chee for reminding him of the fact.

But as he entered his room and glanced at the queen-sized bed, he realized it had never looked quite so empty.

Chapter Three

Much later that night, Leyla sat in front of the television and tried to force her attention on the program on the screen, but her wandering thoughts made it impossible to follow the plot.

Most likely she was going to be fired. After two short days and the trouble she'd taken to move from the res to this ranch, it was all going to be for naught. She'd never been fired from a job before. She'd always made sure that she worked hard, followed orders to a T and never shirked her responsibilities. She was very proud of her work ethic. But this evening she'd let a handsome man with a glib tongue provoke her. She figured Laramie had already phoned Quint Cantrell to let him know he was dissatisfied with the new cook.

Well, there was always a first time for everything, she thought dismally, and she couldn't let it get her down. She'd been in far worst predicaments. Like being in a freezing car, stranded miles away from civilization, with labor pains tearing her right down the middle. Through that ordeal there had been moments when she'd truly believed she and her baby would die. Now, years later, she didn't dwell on those long, fearful hours. Sometimes she drew strength from them. After all, she'd survived and grown stronger from that trial.

With a rueful sigh, she left her seat on the couch and walked into the bedroom where Dillon lay sleeping on a narrow twin bed.

She didn't understand why her son had taken such a liking to Laramie Jones. Up until yesterday, he'd pretty much shunned men in general. Even Dr. Kenoi, who worked at the Apache medical clinic and was known for his ability to connect with children, couldn't get more than five words from Dillon. But five minutes was all it had taken Laramie to have Dillon sitting in his lap and talking up a storm.

Maybe that's why she'd gotten so frustrated with the man. Because she could already see a bond building between him and Dillon. If she allowed him to become attached to the ranch foreman, it would be extremely hard when Reena returned and they had to leave. But how could she purposely step between them without coming across as selfish?

Bending over her son, she brushed her fingers through his hair while doubts and confusion continued to tumble through her mind. Maybe it would be wrong of her to even try to keep Dillon from becoming friends with the man. Her son desperately needed a male influence in his life. Except that he needed a permanent influence. Not one who would be here today and gone tomorrow.

Well, the whole problem was probably going to be taken out of her hands anyway, she thought as she left the bedroom. She'd clearly made Laramie Jones angry and he certainly had the power to see that her job ended.

Too restless to try more television, Leyla walked out of their private suite and into the main part of the house. If she was going to pace around, she might as well have a cup of coffee while she did it.

Before she even reached the doorway of the kitchen she spotted the glow of a light. The sight of it caused her to pause her steps. No one else was in the house except Laramie, so it had to be him in the kitchen. She wasn't keen on facing him again tonight, but if he had plans to get rid of her, then she'd like to know it now instead of later.

Squaring her shoulders, she walked into the room. He said, "I wondered if you were going to keep hovering in the shadows."

He was sitting at the table with a coffee mug in front of him and a piece of the apple pie that had been left over from the night before.

She strode across the tile until she was standing a few steps away from him. "How did you know I was there?" Because his back was to her, she had no idea how he'd detected her presence.

"You're not the only Indian around here."

That surprised her. He had bluish eyes and his skin was no darker than any man's who worked outdoors on a daily basis. But she supposed there could be a hint of Native American blood in his cheekbones and the proud line of his nose.

"You have Indian blood?" she asked.

"I'm told that my mother was Comanche and my father was white. But since I never met either of them, my bloodline is questionable."

Not knowing what to say to that revelation, she walked over to the cabinets and poured herself a mug of coffee.

As she stirred in a splash of cream, he asked, "Are you Apache?"

"Part. From my mother. My father is Navajo."

"Is? I thought you told Bridget and Johnny that your folks were dead."

Her jaw taut, she walked back over to the table and sat at the opposite end from him. "I thought you were a cowboy. Not a misplaced lawyer."

"Just because I straddle a horse for most of the day doesn't make me dumb. I do catch a word here and there once in a while."

There was a thread of sarcasm in his voice and Leyla figured he was still displeased with her. The idea bothered her. Even though the man was chipping away at her peace of mind, she couldn't stop herself from liking him.

"I'm sorry," she said gently. "I didn't mean to sound curt. But Juanita and George Chee are dead to me."

He pushed away his empty pie plate, then turned his head toward her. "Why have you put your parents out of your life? Did they not approve of you having a child out of wedlock?"

Her cheeks were suddenly burning with embarrassment. "My mother was understanding about my situation. But she couldn't stand up to my father's ranting and raving. So to keep peace in my family I left."

"Where was your home?"

"The Navajo reservation up by Farmington."

"Have they ever seen Dillon?" he asked. "Know about him?"

After nearly three years she'd thought the hurt would stop when she thought about Dillon being separated from his grandparents, aunts and uncle. But if anything, it had grown even sharper. The Chee family might not be perfect, but Dillon should be a part of them.

"I've not been back to the Navajo res," she answered his question. "But they know about Dillon. Right after he was born I called my older sister, Zita, and told her. But even if things had been good between us, my parents would never come here. I don't think they've ever been off the res. Besides, the way my father is—I wouldn't want Dillon around him."

He studied her thoughtfully. "Do you think that's fair to your mother?"

"Fair? What's that? Most men take the fairness out of everything," she said flatly. "And my leaving was better for my mother than messing up the life she has left."

"Maybe. But I'm sure losing her daughter has hurt her."

Leyla's head swung dismally back and forth. "Probably so. But you see, my mother is very dependent on my father. And very dutiful. I've never understood why she wants a lazy, domineering husband. Especially when she's the one who works and keeps the bills paid. But that's her business, not mine."

Leaning back in his chair, he sipped his coffee and Leyla tried to focus on her own drink, but it was a chore to make herself swallow. She didn't talk to anyone about her family or her relationship to them. How had this man pulled so many words and emotions from her? What was it about his presence that invited a person to get closer? She couldn't answer those questions. But it was clear that whatever he possessed, she and Dillon were already charmed by it.

He lowered his cup to the tabletop. "Do you have more brothers or sisters than the one you mentioned?"

"I have one brother and two sisters," she said, then decided it was her turn to ask questions. "What about you? Do you have siblings?"

He turned his gaze toward the nearby window and his

profile reminded her of a lone eagle. Fierce and strong, but smart enough to be cautious and wary.

"Like I told you, I didn't know my parents. A few days after I was born, my mother left me with an old rancher and he raised me. He was a bachelor. I was all he had. And he was all I had."

Leyla's family had always been far from perfect. But she had no doubts about her family roots. Even the ones she wasn't proud of. But Laramie didn't know the good or bad or in-between. The realization made her heart ache for him.

"I'm sorry," she softly.

Her gentle remark caused his dark brows to lift with faint surprise. "Don't be. Diego was a good, caring father. When I think back on it I'm amazed that an old bachelor like him raised a baby. I couldn't have done it."

"A person can adapt, even when they believe they can't." Rising to her feet, she walked over to the sink and with her back to him began to rinse the cup. "I suppose you'll be asking Quint to find you another cook now."

"What?"

Forcing herself to turn and face him, she tried to push the words through her thick voice. "I said that I'm sure you'll be asking Quint for a different cook now."

Instead of answering, he rose to his feet. As Leyla watched his long lean frame stride toward her, she felt her heart flutter. He moved with the grace and strength of a dark and dangerous cat. And she suddenly had the feeling that if she tried to run, he'd pounce.

"Why would I be doing that?" he asked in a low, shrewd voice. "Did I say I didn't like your cooking?"

After all Leyla had gone through, she didn't let much of anything or anyone make her nervous. Especially men. As far as she was concerned they weren't worth the emotional toll. But something about Laramie made him different, made her throat thicken, her heart go completely out of sync.

She linked her hands and squeezed to keep them from outwardly trembling. "No. But after the way I talked to you about Dillon, I—"

"Forget it. You were right. Dillon is your son," he said stiffly. "I shouldn't be telling you what he needs. Or doesn't need."

The strained note in his voice compelled her to meet his gaze, and the wounded shadows she saw there did more than confuse her. They touched her in a place that was far too close to her heart. For the past three years she'd tried not to let herself care about anyone or anything except her son. But Laramie was quickly making her realize how very weary she was of holding back her emotions and how very much she wanted to laugh and love again.

"I shouldn't have said those things," she said thickly.

A rueful expression curled up one corner of his lips. "You don't have to say that to keep your job, Leyla."

"My job has nothing to do with apologizing. I'm sorry because I—" Suddenly feeling very trapped and vulnerable, she stepped around him and walked over to the table. A short distance away, huge paned windows exposed a westerly view of the ranch yard. Although it was dark now, the twinkling lights from the barn and connecting corrals made a pretty sight. As she stared at the view, she tried to go on, "You've been nothing but kind to Dillon. And I do realize he needs a man's influence in his life."

"Just not my influence. Is that what you're trying to say in a nice way?"

His question caused her head to jerk around and she watched with dread as he approached her once again. "No! That isn't what I meant," she said, then shrugged with resignation. "Well, maybe I did mean that. But not in a personal way."

Deciding she had to quit letting his nearness put her off, she made herself step toward him until there was no more than a few inches separating them.

He said, "Look, Leyla, you don't have to try to be kind to spare my feelings. I recognize that I'm not a father figure or anything close to it."

He could be, though. From what little interactions she'd seen with him and Dillon, it was obvious to her that he would make a wonderful father. But from what Sassy had told her, the man didn't even date. At least not on a regular or serious basis. And considering he was already in his thirties, that could only mean he hardly had plans to become a father.

She wondered why that was. Because he didn't want a family? Or because he'd never had one?

"If you'd like my opinion, I think you'd make a fine father. It's just that I—" Pausing, she licked her lips and started again. "I don't want Dillon getting too close. We'll have to leave here at some point. If you two become friends, it'll be hard for him to say goodbye."

He frowned. "Do you think that's good for the boy? Don't you think he needs to build relationships with people other than you?"

Knowing there was a measure of guilt and shame in her eyes, she quickly dropped her gaze to the floor. "He does need more than me," she murmured. "But so far no one has stuck around for him. Not his father or his grandfather. And if I can't count on his blood relatives, who can I count on to remain a stable factor in his life?"

"Me," he said solemnly. "And even if you leave, I'll always be right here. Dillon can always come back for visits. You said giving up the cat was a learning experience for him. Well, whether you like it or not, his time here on the Chaparral will be one, too. You need to get ready for that."

Sighing heavily, she lifted her gaze back to him. "I suppose you're right."

"Like I said, I don't know about being a daddy, but I have been a little boy. Being on the ranch gives him a great chance to experience all the animals and see how a cowboy works. Has he ever been on a horse before?"

Leyla practically gasped. "Are you joking? He's not yet three!"

"That's nothing. Quint carried his boys on a horse when they were three months old."

She didn't know what this man was doing to her, but somehow he was opening her eyes and she was beginning to see she needed to let loose. She needed to open her mind from the tiny world she'd boxed around herself and her son. And before she even realized what she was doing, she laid a hand on his forearm and smiled.

"Laramie, I'm not used to ranching life. Dillon isn't the only one who'll be learning. So I—I'll try my best to trust you on these things. And I do want him to make friends. Really."

When Laramie had decided to come down to the kitchen for coffee and pie, this was the last thing he'd expected to happen. As late as it was, he'd been very surprised to see her walking into the room. And even then he'd expected her to give him the frigid treatment. Instead, she'd apologized and now she was actually touching him and smiling with the first genuine warmth he'd seen in her dark eyes. He didn't know what he'd done or said to change her attitude, but whatever it was he was relieved. He was also very, very aware of her softness, the sweet scent of her hair and the seductive curve of her lower lip. The feel of her hand was light and teasing, like a warm gentle breeze slipping over his skin. And he wanted to be closer. Oh, so much closer.

"I'm glad you feel that way, Leyla." His voice sounded husky and intimate, so he cleared his throat before he went on. "Whenever I look at Dillon I see a whole lot of myself. And I want things to be good for him."

"I hope you truly mean that."

"I wouldn't have said it if I didn't."

She turned away from him but not before Laramie caught a bitter sort of resolve in her eyes.

"Dillon's father said plenty of things he didn't mean," she said flatly.

Her words cut into him. It hurt for her to compare him to the bastard who'd deserted her. It also pained him to think what the man's lies must have done to her.

Laramie dared to lay his hand on the back of her shoulder, and the fact that she didn't scurry away filled him with a strange sort of joy. Like when a frightened colt suddenly decided to turn and tiptoe back to his outstretched hand. Trust. Yes, he figured earning Leyla's trust would be a major undertaking.

"Maybe it's time you forget all of that," he said softly.

That turned her back around, and she looked at him with sheer disbelief. "So I can let another man make a fool of me? Oh, no. I won't ever forget."

"The way I see it, you let Dillon's father ruin a part of your life. But there's no sense in letting him ruin the rest of it."

Doubt flickered in her eyes. "Who says I'm letting him ruin anything?"

His hand left her shoulder and slid slowly up the side of her neck until his palm was cradling her jaw. "I do. I see it in your eyes. On your lips. They should be soft and sweet. Instead they're hard and sour."

"And I suppose you think you could make me forget—and soften me up."

Her voice had dropped to a breathy whisper and the sensual sound skittered over his skin like tempting fingertips. He shouldn't be this close to Leyla. And he especially shouldn't be touching her. But it had been a long time since he'd wanted to kiss a woman, to feel her soft curves yielding against him. And like it or not, Leyla touched him in a way that went beyond the physical. He wanted to see past her pretty face and straight to her heart.

"I wouldn't know," he said in a low voice. "Until I tried."

The tight line of her lips fell open and Laramie didn't stop to think. His head swooped, and like a starved man, he fastened his lips over hers.

The initial contact caused her to flinch, but she didn't jerk away, and he was encouraged enough to deepen the pressure of his lips.

Soft, sweet and deliciously warm. The sensations rushed through Laramie like a sudden burst of wind, sweeping away his ability to think about anything except drawing her closer and kissing her until he was completely filled with her.

Just as he was slipping his arms around her waist, the phone he'd left lying on the table began to ring. Laramie desperately wanted to ignore the signal, but Leyla was already pulling away from him.

"You'd better get that," she said in a choked voice, then turned and ran from the room.

Ignoring the phone, Laramie trotted after her. At the doorway leading into her private living quarters, he caught up to her and as his hand closed around her upper arm, she whirled back to him.

"Forget the phone," he muttered. "I want to talk to you first."

With her gaze focused rigidly away from him, she said, "There's nothing to talk about. I let you push me into behaving recklessly!" Her gaze swept up to his face and this time there was a fierceness in the dark brown depths. "I won't let that happen again!"

"Kissing me makes you reckless, huh? Then what does it make me? A fool for thinking you might actually be a woman with a woman's feelings?"

Clearly furious, she jerked away from his grasp and slammed the door in his face.

Laramie instantly raised his hand to pound on the wooden partition, but he let it drop. The last thing he wanted to do was wake Dillon. The boy didn't need to see his mother upset.

With a rueful sigh, he turned away from the door and started back to the kitchen. He'd already done and said far too much tonight. And the phone call was probably from someone who needed him to deal with something. Being the manager of this huge ranch always kept him in demand. But just for once Laramie would like to think he was needed by a woman. Especially a woman with long black hair and dark wounded eyes.

When Leyla entered the kitchen early the next morning, she found a note from Laramie fastened to the refrigerator. He'd had to leave the house early so there was no need to prepare his breakfast, but he did plan to be back for supper.

Leyla didn't know it was possible to feel disappointment and relief at the same time, but as she crumpled the note and tossed it into the trash, the conflicting emotions did a good job of confusing her. But then so had his kiss last night. The touch of his lips had swept her away and filled her with longing. She'd wanted it to go on forever, but somehow, some way, sanity had prevailed and given her enough strength to pull away from him. But what about the next time? How could she possibly resist the man?

Trying to shove away her worrisome thoughts, she made coffee, then prepared a pot of oatmeal for Dillon and herself. The child would be up soon and no doubt would race here to the kitchen to see if Laramie was around.

Last night, before he'd gone to sleep, he plied her with questions about the man. The last one being did he have a little boy, too.

Even now the question dug at her in places she'd believed she'd shut the door on long ago. It was still hard for her to fathom the idea that Laramie's mother had left her newborn. Had the woman meant to come back but for some reason couldn't? If she wasn't dead, why had she left her son behind to be raised by someone who'd not even been a relative?

Laramie had said that when he looked at Dillon he saw a bit of himself. That had touched her. She'd not expected anything like that from the rancher. In fact, she'd never expected him to take any sort of notice of her or Dillon. But already he'd kissed her senseless and promised to be a friend to Dillon. Oh, God, where was it all going to end? When Reena came back and she and Dillon were forced to leave, that's where it would end, she thought dismally.

You can always bring him back for visits.

Visits were not what she and Dillon needed. They needed a home they could call theirs, a place that no one could take away from them. And she needed to get on with her education to make those dreams come true. And later, maybe years later, she'd be in a stable position where she could allow a man to come into their lives.

* * *

After breakfast, Dillon was sitting on the floor playing with a set of farm animals while Leyla finished the last of her coffee when the phone on the breakfast bar rang.

When Sassy was around, Leyla always let her take the calls, but the other woman hadn't yet arrived to work, so she hurried over to the bar and picked up the receiver.

"Chaparral ranch," she answered.

"Leyla, it's Reena. I was just calling to make sure everything is going okay."

"Everything is fine." Except that the sexy ranch foreman had gotten under her skin, Leyla thought with a measure of frustration.

"Good. I also forgot to tell you that whenever you're in town shopping for the ranch, you're perfectly welcome to use the credit card for things you might need for yourself."

Leyla couldn't imagine charging any sort of personal expense to the ranch. She was fiercely independent and made it a rule to never ask for anything more than her salary. "I wouldn't dream of taking advantage like that."

Reena chuckled. "Leyla, I wasn't suggesting you go out and buy diamonds or mink. I'm talking about basic necessities that a woman needs. Those are considered part of your working expenses."

"Thank you, Reena, but I hardly need a thing. This place is a mansion. Especially after living in my aunt's house on the res. The roof leaks when it rains or the snow starts to melt and the water pipes only work in the bathroom. So you see, I have more than plenty."

Reena paused for a moment, and Leyla figured the description of her aunt's house had taken the other woman aback.

After a moment, she said, "I'm glad you got the chance to enjoy the Chaparral, Leyla. And I want you to feel at home. Laramie is very special to me. And I know you'll take extra good care of him."

Leyla wondered what the cook would think if she knew exactly how good she'd taken care of Laramie last night. Just the memory of his hard lips rocking over hers was enough to send a shock of heat through her body. And she was still asking herself why she'd allowed the kiss to happen.

"Don't worry, Reena. I promise to take care of your rooms and not let Dillon break anything. And Laramie doesn't seem picky about what he eats. I don't think I'll have any problems with him." At least not with the cooking part of her job, she thought. "Uh, Reena, this morning when I came down to the kitchen he was already gone. That was five o'clock. Do I need to make breakfast earlier?"

Reena chuckled. "Don't worry about getting up with the roosters. Some mornings Laramie has to be out very early. He'll find something for himself or eat at the bunkhouse."

Leyla's thoughts rolled back two nights ago when she'd met him for the very first time. He'd looked saddle-weary. And she suspected that while she was here on the ranch, she would see him in that condition more often than not. He worked very hard. Just not for himself. That didn't make sense to her. The Cantrells trusted him to run their family business. That meant he was top-notch at his job. A man with that much talent could be using it on a ranch of his own. But maybe Laramie didn't want a home of his own, she thought. No more than he appeared to want a family.

Trying to push the nagging thoughts of Laramie away, she asked, "How are things going for you at Apache Wells?"

"The Chaparral has been my home for forty years, so

it feels very strange to be away from it," Reena admitted. "But Abe is a sweetheart, so I can hardly complain."

A sweetheart? That seemed like an odd term for the cook to be using for her employer. "Sassy told me the man is a crotchety old thing."

Reena laughed and Leyla could detect a sense of deep affection in the sound. Maybe the term "sweetheart" wasn't so odd after all, she thought.

The cook said, "Sassy is too young to appreciate a man like Abe. As far as that goes, Sassy wouldn't know a good man if one walked right under her nose."

"She's very sweet, though," Leyla defended the maid.

"And so are you," Reena said kindly.

The two women talked for a brief moment more and then Reena ended the call. As Leyla hung up the phone, she wondered if the cook knew anything about Laramie's parents and what might have happened to them.

Stop it, Leyla! Forget that the man grew up without his real parents. Forget the way he looked at you, touched you. And most of all push that kiss of his from your mind.

When Laramie trudged his way through the atrium and into the kitchen that night, it was well past ten. Except for a night-light burning over the cabinet counter, the room was dark and empty. At this hour, he'd not expected Leyla to be up and waiting, but he'd found himself hoping she would be. In fact, he'd spent the whole damned day thinking about the woman and that kiss. And that irritated the heck out of him. With one problem after another popping up on the ranch, his mind needed to be on work, not a lovely little woman with sweet-tasting lips.

He scrubbed his hands at the sink, then pulled out the warming drawer at the bottom of the gas range. Inside he found a plate of smothered meat, a bowl of seasoned potatoes and another with candied carrots.

He ate the meal quickly, then rinsed the dishes and placed them in the dishwasher. He planned to shower and go straight to bed, so he dismissed the idea of having coffee and dessert and left the kitchen to go upstairs to his room.

On the way through the dark, he was passing the door to Leyla's living quarters when it suddenly swung open, nearly hitting him in the face.

"Oh, hell!"

"Laramie!"

Their words came out at the same time and it was obvious to Laramie that she'd not had any idea that he was in the house, much less that her door was about to slam him in the nose. For a second night in a row.

"I didn't know you were back," she said with concern. "Did I hit you with the door?"

She'd not seemed too worried about slamming him in the face last night, he thought wryly. "No. You just startled me, that's all."

Even though the small hallway was illuminated dimly, Laramie could see she was wearing a robe made of something soft and blue. It was tied at the waist and the V of the neck dipped low to a spot between her breasts. Her long hair had been loosened from its knot and now lay like a shiny piece of satin upon her shoulders. She looked more than pretty, he decided—she looked downright sexy.

"I thought I'd check the kitchen to see if you'd eaten so that I could put away the dishes."

"No need for you to bother. I've already put everything away."

Her lips pursed with disapproval. "That's not good. That's my job."

"It was nothing," he assured her. "Thanks for the supper."

"That's why I'm here. Just to prepare your meals."

Her remark jerked his wandering thoughts back to reality. She was here to cook for him, not to seduce him. She wasn't here to make him dream about things that were out of his reach. She wasn't here to turn him into some sort of lovesick fool.

"Yeah," he said, "Reena used to cook for the whole Cantrell family. Nowadays it's mostly just me here since Frankie is staying with her sons in Texas."

"And they keep Reena on the payroll just to cook for you?"

He shook his head. "It's not that simple. Reena has been here for so long that she's part of the family. And she still wants to contribute to the ranch. This is her home, too, so cooking for me gives her a reason to keep working." He didn't add that he'd told Quint outright that he could prepare his own meals or eat with the men in the bunkhouse. More than anything he wanted Leyla to think she was needed. Besides, the more he thought about it, the more he'd decided that Quint had hired Leyla more as a way to help her than to provide Laramie with a cook.

"I see. The Cantrells must be very loyal to their employees."

"After you've been here a while you'll understand just how loyal they are," he told her, while thinking there was no reason for him to keep lingering. He should tell her a quick good-night and be on his way. But everything inside of him was screaming to stay put and drink in the lovely sight of her just a bit longer.

She nervously clasped her hands in front of her. "Well, about last night—I'm sorry I behaved so badly. And I wanted you to know that I was more angry at myself than you."

He was surprised that she'd brought the incident up. He'd expected her to be cold and quiet about the whole matter.

"Hmm. You could have fooled me. But I'm the one to blame, Leyla. I shouldn't have kissed you." He couldn't stop himself from moving closer and as he looked down at her, his fingers ached to touch the smooth brown skin exposed by the robe, to press his lips against the throbbing pulse at the base of her neck. "But I'm not sorry I did."

She swallowed, and he could see that his remark troubled her. As his gaze traveled over her face, he realized how very much he wanted to pull her into his arms, to assure her that he wasn't like the man who'd gotten her pregnant and then walked out. That he wasn't a man she needed to fear.

"I'm not—it's nothing personal, Laramie, but I—" She turned slightly away from him and stared into the darkness of the hallway. "Well, I have plans for Dillon and me. And I'm just not sure I'm ready to let another man into my life just yet."

In spite of her words, he reached out and snared a shiny strand of her hair between his fingers. "I haven't been picturing a woman in my future, either," he said huskily. "I doubt that I'm the family type, Leyla. My friends all have wives and children and I see how fortunate they are to have each other. But I wasn't raised in a family environment. And I figure a husband or father isn't something that should be done on a trial basis. But that doesn't mean I don't want or need to be loved. And I have a feeling that you want and need that just as much as I do."

Swallowing again, she turned her gaze back to his. "You accused me of being unfeeling. But that's not true. I'm just like any other woman—I want to be loved. But I want it to be right and true. I don't want to make another mistake."

He wrapped his hands over her shoulders and the warmth of her flesh spread through the fabric to his fingers. "I understand that, Leyla. And you need to understand that you don't have to worry about me hurting you."

An anguished look came over her face and then she shook her head. "You're wrong, Laramie. I'm already worried. Because I'm beginning to like you...very much."

Her words pierced his chest and landed right in the center of his heart. "Oh, Leyla," he said in a hoarse whisper, "I'm beginning to like you very much, too."

Before he could say or do something he might totally regret in the morning, he bent and placed a tiny kiss on her cheek.

"Good night," he murmured.

Dropping his hold on her shoulders, he turned and quickly strode to the stairs. As he climbed them two at a time, he heard Leyla's door close firmly behind her.

Chapter Four

Because Leyla had started to work in the middle of the week, the next day was Saturday. Reena had warned her that, more often than not, Laramie worked seven days a week. But on Sundays he would fend for himself, so a cook wouldn't need to be on duty.

This morning Leyla was already in the kitchen mixing biscuits when he entered the kitchen dressed in work gear with his black hat pulled low over his forehead and spurs jingling with each long stride he took. Expecting him to go straight to the coffee machine, it surprised her to see him heading for the door instead.

"Sorry, Leyla. I don't have time for breakfast this morning. I just got word of an emergency. You might as well take the day off, 'cause I don't know when I'll be back."

"Okay. Thank you," she said, but she doubted he heard her words as he was already hurrying out the door.

It wasn't until later in the day that Sassy managed to

find out from one of the ranch hands what the emergency was all about. Early this morning before daylight, a horse wrangler had discovered two of the ranch's prize cutting horses missing. Now practically every cowboy on the place was out looking for them.

"If you ask me, there's a traitor among us," Sassy said as she sipped from a tall glass of iced tea.

"What do you mean? You think someone on the ranch took the horses?" Leyla asked the other woman.

The redhead grimaced. "Listen, if you've ever been down to the horse barn, you'd see it would be pretty nigh impossible for two horses to work their way past several gates. Some of them are Houdinis at slipping latches but not that many latches."

The two women were seated at the kitchen table and Leyla could hardly keep her gaze away from the distant view of the ranch yard. Shortly after daylight there had been a flurry of activity around the barns. Now practically nothing was going on and both women presumed all the ranch hands were gone on the search for the valuable horses.

"That would be awful to think that someone on the ranch would steal or cause mischief. Do the barns have guards?"

"Sure do. That's why I think it's an inside job." Wrinkling her nose, she rose to her feet. "You can bet Laramie is fit to be tied. The horses on this place are his babies."

Seeing the troubled look on Laramie's face this morning as he'd hurried out the door had knocked Leyla off-kilter. Up until today, she'd not really thought of him as a man who had worries. He was such a strong, able-bodied man that it seemed like he should be able to ward off any sort of problem before it ever got near him. The incident today had shown Leyla he was human just like everyone else. The notion softened her heart and had her wishing that she could make everything right for him.

"His babies. Why do you say that? Does he own them?" she asked Sassy.

The maid carried her tea glass over to the sink and dumped the dregs of her drink. "Before Laramie was promoted to foreman, he managed the ranch's horse stock. As far as that goes, he still does. As for him owning them, I think he has a few of his own personal horses in the bunch. I'm not sure about the ones that went missing today."

With one last glance toward the ranch yard, Leyla rose to her feet and walked over to where Sassy was washing her glass.

"If someone did take the horses or even let them escape, that might mean the person had a grudge against Laramie or someone here on the ranch. That's a scary notion."

Sassy dried the glass and placed it in the cabinet. "Yeah, well, this kind of stuff can't keep going on forever." Turning toward Leyla she smiled impishly. "Let's forget all that worrisome stuff. I'm finished for the day and you don't have a thing to do, either. Let's go to town and do some shopping."

Leyla had never been one to do the girlfriend thing. Mostly because she'd come to Lincoln County not knowing anyone except her aunt Oneida. And it took money to go on any sort of outings, especially those that involved shopping. "Shopping? It's very friendly of you to invite me, Sassy, but I don't think so. I'm trying to save my money."

Sassy frowned with disapproval. "That's well and good. But a girl has to have a little break from work once in a while. And you don't have to spend any money. I'll drive and you can just window-shop if you want. What do you say? It'll be fun."

Fun? Leyla couldn't remember the last time she'd actually had fun. From the moment she'd discovered she was pregnant with Heath's child, entertainment and carefree pleasures had gone out of her life. Now, she didn't look for those things. Her days were all about being practical and surviving on her own.

"I'd have to take Dillon. And you don't want your afternoon saddled with the two of us," Leyla reasoned.

With a hand on Leyla's shoulder, Sassy urged her out of the kitchen. "Go get ready. I'll meet you and Dillon on the front porch in ten minutes. And if you don't show up, I'll come after you," the maid warned.

Fifteen minutes later the two women were traveling in Sassy's truck with Dillon safely belted between them in a booster seat. The unexpected trip had brought a bright shine to her son's eyes and Sassy kept him giggling with silly stories about animals that could talk to a little boy who looked amazingly like him.

Leyla was glad that her son was enjoying himself. But her thoughts continued to dwell on Laramie. "I feel guilty about leaving the ranch," she told Sassy. "Especially with the trouble that's happened."

Sassy batted a dismissive hand through the air. "Don't be silly, Leyla. You can't do anything about the missing horses. Besides, you said Laramie gave you the day off."

Leyla sighed. "He did. But, well, going out like this makes me seem indifferent."

"Listen, Leyla, you can't fix Laramie's problems. And…" Her words came to an abrupt end as she glanced across the truck seat at Leyla. "You're worried about him, aren't you?"

Pink heat rushed up Leyla's neck and onto her cheeks. "A little," she admitted. "So far he's been very kind to me and Dillon. And I want things to go well for him."

"Oh. I see," Sassy said shrewdly.

"What do you see?"

The maid suddenly shrugged one shoulder in a casual way. "Nothing. Except that you're very kindhearted, Leyla." By now the two women had reached the highway and Sassy glanced at her before she pulled onto the two-lane asphalt. "I know I said I wouldn't mention—uh—" For Dillon's sake, she chose her next words carefully. "Your old boyfriend. But I'm just curious. Was he a nice guy—I mean, in the beginning?"

Sighing, Leyla turned her gaze toward the window. "In the beginning Heath treated me like a princess." Looking over at Sassy, she smiled cynically. "That should have been a red flag. Like you said—when a girl starts thinking she's a princess and her man is a prince, she's already in trouble. Why do you ask?"

Sassy's smile was thoughtful. "When it comes to men, a girl needs all the pointers she can get."

"Do you have a boyfriend right now?" Leyla asked curiously.

The smile on her lips pressed into a flat line. "Not one I'd want to have a baby with. But there is one who— Well, I'd give him the world if I could. Trouble is, he looks right past me."

When the two women reached the town of Ruidoso they both agreed a hamburger at the Blue Mesa, where Leyla used to work, would be a treat, and Dillon especially liked sitting at an outside table to eat their lunch. After the meal, the two women strolled along the busy shops that lined the main thoroughfare through the resort town.

Leyla kept her purchases to a single card of hairpins for herself and a small stuffed animal in the shape of a horse for Dillon. Before they left town, Sassy was kind enough to stop by the nursing home to let Leyla visit her aunt.

Oneida was in her late seventies. The stroke she'd suffered nearly three years ago had affected her right side but thankfully not her ability to speak. Therapy was helping her learn to walk again and she was making far more progress than Leyla would have thought possible for a person her age.

When Leyla entered the stark room, her aunt was sitting in a cushioned chair watching a game show on a small television set. As soon as she spotted Leyla, her face split into a happy smile.

"My sweet girl. I didn't expect to see you this soon."

Leyla pressed a kiss on her aunt's wrinkled forehead, then took a seat on the side of the small bed. "My friend brought me to town and I wanted to see you before we drove home."

The woman muted the sound on the television. "That's good. And where is Dillon?"

"He's outside with her. Playing on the lawn."

"So how is your new job? One of the nurses tells me that the ranch is owned by very rich people. That they even own a gold mine."

"That's true. But that has nothing to do with me. I only cook for one man. The manager of the ranch."

"Maybe this job will turn into something permanent," Oneida said hopefully. "It would make me happy to know that you have a roof over your head that doesn't leak."

Leyla closed her hand around Oneida's bony one. "Oh, Auntie, I want to get a place of my own where you can live with us, too. It will take time, but I will get it."

Smiling wanly, the woman patted the top of Leyla's hand. "You are a good girl. But you could never take care of me. Not like I am now."

"Every day you're getting better. And Dillon and I need you. Much more than you know. If it hadn't been for you…" Biting her lip, she looked away so that her aunt couldn't see the moisture in her eyes. After all this time she didn't know why she still got emotional about being separated from her family, but she did. "Well, you gave me a home. You've loved me when I didn't have anyone else. I won't forget that."

Oneida patted her hand again. "When my sister married George, she lost her soul. She was so weak that she handed it over to him. You're not going to be like her, though. I never worry about that. You took after me. Not her."

To her aunt's credit, she'd married a respectable man who'd worked hard to give his wife a decent life. Unfortunately they were never able to have children and then he was killed in a car accident involving a drunk driver. Left alone, Oneida had worked as long as her health had allowed. And afterward she'd done the best she could on a meager fixed income. The woman had little in the way of material things, but she had her pride and faith, and she was basically happy. That was more than Leyla's mother had.

"Do you need anything, Auntie? I'll get paid next week. I can bring whatever you need back to you then."

Smiling gently, Oneida shook her head. "Not a thing, honey. Just seeing your pretty face is enough. Now tell me about my nephew. What does he think about the ranch?"

It wasn't so much as what Dillon thought about the ranch as it was what he thought about the man who ran it. But she wasn't going to say anything about Laramie to her aunt. He wasn't that important. She wasn't going to let him be.

"He seems happy. The owner's grandsons have lots of toys stored at the house and Dillon is allowed to play with them. And there's a nice yard with a huge gym set. From the house he can see the horses and cows, and he keeps pestering me to take him to down to the ranch yard to see them. So I'm taking extra care to see that he doesn't wander off down there on his own."

"He's a typical boy. Let him see and learn. You'll know when and how to let him do things. You're a good mother."

Leyla shook her head with disbelief. "I don't know why you always have such confidence in me. I made terrible mistakes with Dillon's father."

A smug look came over the woman's wrinkled face. "Maybe that's why I do have such faith in you. Because I know you've learned. You won't make those kind of mistakes again."

She'd learned all right, Leyla thought. But what had it done to her? Laramie had described her as unfeeling. Sassy implied she was wasting herself. That wasn't the person she wanted to be. She wanted everyone to see that Heath hadn't crushed the loving person deep inside her.

Leyla talked for a few more minutes with Oneida, then said her goodbyes. Outside, Sassy and Dillon were watching a pair of squirrels scamper up and down a nearby tree.

As Leyla approached the bench, she asked Sassy, "How in the world did you get him to sit like that?"

The other woman laughed. "It wasn't my mothering skills, I can tell you that much. He's enamored with the squirrels."

Taking Dillon by the hand, Leyla urged her son away from the bench and the chattering squirrels. After all of them were safely buckled in the truck, Sassy backed onto the quiet street and turned in the direction that would lead them out of town.

"How's your aunt?" Sassy asked as she maneuvered the truck through heavier traffic.

Leyla smiled. "Slowly improving. She's able to dress herself now and walk with a walker." The sight of the nursing home in her side mirror strengthened her resolve to make things better for her aunt. "Her doctor says she might be able to come home in a few months. Since her house has become practically unlivable I'm going to find us a more decent place to live."

"You were living in that house a few days ago," Sassy pointed out.

"That's true. But Oneida is frail. She needs to be cool in summer and warm in winter, with hot water in the bathroom and kitchen."

"Sounds like she'll need help."

"I'm the only help she has. So I've been planning to rent a house for the three of us. Oneida hates being in town, so that means I'll have to find something on the res."

"That's taking on a big load," Sassy said thoughtfully. "Wouldn't you rather stay on the Chaparral and find a caretaker for your aunt?"

Even as Leyla shook her head, images of Laramie were dancing through her mind. Once her job on the ranch was over, she'd probably never see him again. It was a lonely thought.

"I don't have that choice, Sassy. Once Reena returns, my job will be over. Besides, Oneida gave me a home when I desperately needed somewhere to live. I won't push her aside. I love her."

"Hmm. I'm sure Quint could find another job for you on the ranch, and they always have some sort of empty housing available for employees who need it. You could take Oneida out there to live with you. The general office always needs help. The regular bookkeeper has been with them for about four years, but the staff under her is always turning over. There aren't many women who want to make the long, rough drive out to the ranch. It doesn't take long for the trek to turn a car into a piece of junk. And many people don't want to live out there in the wilds, either."

Leyla countered. "You make the drive every day instead of living out there."

"I live in town for a reason. And this old truck of mine makes the drive just fine," Sassy joked.

A wan smile touched Leyla's lips. "Well, I'll be leaving. The ranch isn't for me, either."

Sassy frowned. "You sure as heck fooled me. I thought you fit right in."

To fit in and be a part of a family was something Leyla had always wanted. And she was already growing to love the Chaparral. But her job was temporary and from what Laramie had told her, he wasn't looking for a woman to be a permanent part of his life. To believe she could make her home there would only be wishful thinking.

Inside the vet's office on the Chaparral, Russ poured two mugs full of coffee and handed one to Laramie before he took a seat behind his desk. With both hands gripping the mug, Laramie sank wearily into a nearby armchair.

"Your mare came out of the surgery just fine," Russ told him. "But that was a damned nasty cut on her ankle. Laurel is finishing the bandage now. Once she wakes up well enough to walk, you can take her back to her stall. Just be sure to tell the boys to keep the space as clean as possible. We'll change her bandage in a few days, but not before."

"I would take somebody's head off for this," Laramie muttered angrily. "If I just knew who."

He and practically every ranch hand on the place had covered miles of rough terrain before they'd finally spotted the pregnant mare and yearling colt in a washed-out draw several miles away from the ranch yard. The mare had suffered a deep ankle cut that had required surgery to repair.

"Just be glad you found them," the vet said in an effort to smooth Laramie's feathers. "And the mare will survive. That's something to be thankful for."

"I am thankful," Laramie grumbled. "But you and I both know that her ankle will be scarred for the rest of her life."

"Well, it's not like she was up for sale. Having a scarred ankle won't keep her from producing nice foals."

"Yes, but it dropped her worth several thousands of dollars," he shot back at Russ. "And the idiot who let them out of the barn ought to pay. If nothing else, they should pay for being so ignorant!"

Russ sipped his coffee, then turned a pointed look on Laramie. "Who said it was ignorance that caused the horses to get loose?"

Laramie narrowed his eyes as he contemplated the vet's question. "You think this whole thing is more than a dumb mistake by a ranch hand who doesn't want to own up to it?"

Russ nodded. "Look, ever since I discovered that Josie's milk had been tainted, I have thought evil is lurking among us."

Josie was one of twin calves born at the end of the winter. Laurel had been raising her on a bottle, and during that time the calf had become deathly ill. It was later learned that the goat's milk had been tainted with some sort of toxin. So far no one knew how it had gotten in the milk. But clearly Russ hadn't forgotten the incident.

"That's a bold statement," Laramie said.

"I meant for it to be."

"Thank God none of the cattle or horses have gotten sick since Josie."

"That's true. But look at the machinery that's broken down. The tractor. The grain truck. The water pump that supplies the feed lots. The two windmills on the west range."

"Yeah, and missing horses on two different occasions," Laramie added with disgust. "Damn it, Russ, at times every ranch runs through a rash of problems. I keep trying to tell myself that's what is happening around here."

"I don't think you believe that any more than I do," Russ said.

Rising from the chair, he wandered restlessly around the plush office. "I know one thing—it makes me look as worthless as hell."

"That's crazy. You're not causing these problems. Besides, you're like the salt of the earth around here. You don't need to prove yourself to anybody and especially not the Cantrells."

No. The Cantrell family had always entrusted Laramie with things they regarded important. They believed in him and his ability to deal with matters and problems in a strong, decisive way. But it wasn't the Cantrells' opinion of him that he was worried about. It was Leyla's.

Laramie didn't know why he wanted to impress the young cook. Sure, he found her attractive, but he'd not gone sappy over the woman. She was a temporary fixture on the Chaparral. He couldn't let himself get sappy, he quickly reminded himself.

The door connecting the inner barn to the office suddenly opened and Laramie looked over his shoulder to see Russ's wife entering the room.

Even though her midsection was rounded with child, the woman was still continuing to work with an energy that amazed Laramie. Seeing both Laurel and Maura pregnant and working often had him wondering about his own mother. Diego had told him that Peggy had worked as a waitress in an Alto café right up until the time she'd given birth to him. That couldn't have been easy and Laramie had often wished he could find the woman. Not to judge her for leaving him behind, but to thank her for not terminating her pregnancy and to ask her why she'd never returned for him.

"Junebug is awake and standing," she told the two men. "She's putting weight on that ankle. But she's so full of painkillers right now she probably doesn't know it's sore."

"And for the next few days we don't want her to feel that soreness," Russ told her, then motioned to Laramie. "Let's go see if she can make it back to her stall okay."

A little more than an hour later, Leyla was getting ready for bed when she heard Laramie walking through the hallway toward the staircase.

Telling herself she needed to make sure he wasn't hungry, she jerked on her robe and hurried out of her suite of rooms to intercept him.

"Laramie?" she called just as he was about to disappear through a doorway several feet down from hers.

Upon hearing her voice, he paused, then walked slowly back to where she stood by her door.

"Hello, Leyla."

If she'd thought he looked weary that first evening she'd met him, he looked downright exhausted now. Lines of fatigue marred his face, and the front of his shirt and one of his sleeves appeared to be smeared with dried blood.

Feeling extremely foolish, she said, "You're very tired. I shouldn't have bothered you."

He stepped closer. "You're not bothering me. Is anything wrong?"

"No. I—" She paused as she resisted the urge to clutch the edges of her robe together at her throat. "I was worried. Sassy said your horses had gone missing. Did you find them?"

The tension around his mouth eased slightly. "Found them right about sundown. The mare was injured and the vet just now finished suturing her ankle."

That would explain the blood on his shirt, Leyla thought. Compassion for him and the animal caused her to groan out loud. "Oh, no. Is she going to be okay?"

"Let's put it this way—she'll live. But her injury is like a beautiful woman such as yourself getting an ugly scar on her face that will never go away."

"I'm so sorry."

A lopsided grin touched his lips. "I think you really mean that."

Slightly offended by his remark, she said, "I do. I love animals."

His gaze swept curiously over her face before it fell to the watch on his wrist. "I realize it's pretty late and I gave you the day off. But since you're still up, do you have anything in the refrigerator I can eat?"

The fact that he was asking so nicely instead of ordering her like an employee made her feel special and before she could stop herself she was smiling at him.

"There are plenty of leftovers," she told him. "I'll heat them for you."

He said, "Great. Just let me get a quick shower and I'll be right down."

Leyla watched him stride away, then turned and hurried back into her apartment. After checking to make sure Dillon was still sound asleep, Leyla glanced down at her blue satin robe. She should probably change back into her jeans and shirt, but she'd already put them into the dirty laundry bin and she didn't want to take the time to dig out more clothes when the robe adequately covered her.

Besides, none of that mattered. All that mattered was that Laramie was home and safe. That had her heart smiling and her bare feet skimming over the tiles as she raced to the kitchen.

You've lost it, Leyla. You're letting yourself get all besotted by a man again.

The little warning voice in her head caused her footsteps to slow but only for a moment. She wasn't becoming infatuated with Laramie Jones, she fiercely argued with herself. She was simply letting herself feel like a woman again. And that was hardly a crime of passion.

Chapter Five

By the time Laramie reappeared, she had everything heated and ready for him to eat.

As he sank into a chair at the end of the kitchen table, he said, "This is very nice of you, Leyla." Reaching for a plate of pork chops, he glanced around the kitchen. "Is Dillon already asleep for the night?"

"Yes. He goes to bed at eight-thirty or nine and won't wake until about six."

"I can't remember ever getting that much sleep." He forked the meat on his plate, then reached for a bowl of Spanish rice. "I had planned to take Dillon down to the barns today to see the horses and cows. But the ordeal with the missing horses came up."

That meant Leyla would've had to accompany him and Dillon, she thought. And spending more time with Laramie might not be a smart thing to do. But she couldn't help but feel a little disappointed that she'd missed the chance.

She sank into a chair to his right. "Dillon would have liked that," she told him. "But we had a busy day anyway. We went to town with Sassy. She wanted to go shopping. I mostly looked."

"That doesn't surprise me—that you mostly looked," he added knowingly.

Leyla glanced down at herself as a blush worked its way to her face. Her clothes were plain, many of them coming from local thrift shops. And the only good piece of jewelry she possessed was a pair of silver earrings that her mother had given her for her sixteenth birthday. The little dangling doves only left Leyla's ears when she went to bed at night.

"I guess it's easy to see that I can't buy the latest fashions," she said.

His quiet laugh caught her off guard.

"If you waltzed through this kitchen wearing the latest fashion, I wouldn't know it. Besides," he added with an appreciative glance at her, "you don't need special clothes to look nice."

He might call himself just a cowboy, but he definitely knew what a woman wants to hear, she thought.

"Well, I have what's important to me." Looking over at him, she allowed herself to gaze at his dark, rugged features. A shadow of a beard covered his chin and jaws, and faint, crescent-shaped lines were etched beneath his eyes. He'd been going since before sunup, but she figured the stress of the lost horses had worn him down more than the physical energy it had taken to find them. "Sassy believes someone here at the ranch let your horses loose. Is that what you think?"

His lips pressed into a tight line. "Believe me, Sassy isn't the only one saying those things. But I'm not going to jump to conclusions or presume anything—yet."

There was a note of annoyance in his voice, and she figured the questions being gossiped about on the ranch bothered him greatly. As manager, the ranch was a reflection of his work. And his work was clearly his life.

"Maybe the sheriff's department should investigate."

"Quint's brother-in-law *is* the Undersheriff. But we can't call Brady Donovan unless, God forbid, something more concrete happens. Up until now it's all just fishy assumptions. And the Lincoln County Sheriff's Department has more important things to do than go chasing after suspicions."

"Yes. I suppose you are right."

He glanced at her and the hardness in his eyes yielded to a soft look of concern. "You aren't frightened to be living here, are you? I know it's twenty miles from town and the nearest neighbor is Tyler Pickens and he's at least five miles away, but we do have our own security in and around the ranch yard."

"Yes, Sassy said there were guards at the barns. She's never mentioned a neighbor, though. Does he have a connection to the Chaparral?"

Laramie shook his head. "Not at all. About ten years ago he bought the land next to this ranch and hauled in a huge herd of Polled Herefords. Since then he's pretty much kept to himself. I don't think he likes people. But the feeling is mutual, I think. Most people don't like him. The men who work for him say he's tough but fair-minded and that's about all they have to say. Quint and I leave him alone and he leaves us alone."

"Some people are just more comfortable being alone."

Seeing he was nearly finished with the food on his plate, she left the table and went to start a fresh pot of coffee.

As she filled the machine with cold water, he said,

"Well, I hope you don't mind being alone because I'm going to be away from the house for the next week."

Taken by complete surprise, she whirled around and fixed him with a blank stare. "Gone? Where?"

"Spring roundup starts Monday. That's always a very busy time here on the ranch. We gather all the new calves for branding and vaccinations and things like that."

"And that takes more than one day?" She could see that her question amused him, and she frowned at him. "Laramie, I don't know about cattle ranches. Especially one this big."

The thought of him being gone for several days had practically jerked her feet out from under her. Even though he had an erratic schedule and she didn't always see him, she still knew he was in the house at night, that if she needed him he'd be there. Funny how quickly she'd come to count on his presence. And not for safety reasons, either.

"Sorry, Leyla. I guess I've done this sort of thing for so long that it's all second nature to me. I forget that not everyone knows about raising cattle. But yeah, it will take five, six, sometimes even seven days. Depending on how things go. With the spring being mild, we'll probably have to go higher into the mountains and drive down some of the cow/calf pairs. That takes more time than gathering the valley calves."

With the coffee brewing, she walked back over to the table. As she grew closer to him, she could feel his gaze darting over her. That was all it took to fill her whole body with uncomfortable heat.

"So you won't be coming here to the house at all next week? Where will you eat and sleep?"

"I'll try to make it back to the ranch a few times during the week. It just depends on how things are going with roundup. The rest of the time, I'll be sleeping on the ground on bedrolls and eating off the chuck wagon with the rest of the men. The Chaparral does roundup just like the early ranches did more than a hundred years ago. We've kept that tradition all this time."

It pleased her that he considered her intelligent enough to appreciate his work and the history connected to it. Most of the men she encountered at her former job looked at her as a sex object with no ability to think past the length of her nose. Laramie treated her differently.

"Once, when I was working at the Blue Mesa I overheard a pair of ranchers arguing about whether to use horses or four-wheelers to gather their cattle. I didn't understand what all the fuss was about, but the man who preferred horses got very heated about it all. I thought they were going to come to blows. I actually wanted to dump hot coffee on both their heads," she admitted. "But now that I'm living out here, I see the advantage of doing things on horseback. The terrain is very rough."

He nodded. "Only a horse can take us to the rugged spots we need to go. And it's a proven fact that cows handled by men on horseback are much less stressed."

"Guess it makes sense that another animal moving among them feels more comfortable than a roaring, smelly machine," she said thoughtfully.

He grinned at her. "My, my. I do think you're catching on to all of this ranching stuff, Miss Chee."

The sensual, teasing curve to his lips had her thoughts straying back to the kiss he'd given her. She'd been shocked at how much she'd wanted to go on kissing him. How much she'd wanted to wrap her arms around him and keep holding on. The memory of those moments had never left her. Even worse, she longed to repeat them.

Clearing her throat, she said, "Between you and Sassy

I'm learning." Before he could make a reply to that, she hurried over to the cabinet to fetch the coffee.

Moments later, she returned to the table with a steaming mug and a saucer full of fig wafers. "I'm sorry," she told him, "but you'll have to make do tonight with Dillon's favorite dessert. Because you gave me the day off, I didn't do any baking."

"If fig cookies are good enough for Dillon, then they're good for me," he said. "I wish it wasn't so late and he could eat some with me."

Dillon needs a daddy.

Now why was Sassy's remark haunting her now? Leyla wondered. Laramie Jones wasn't a daddy type of man. He had all the makings, but he didn't want that for himself. No, if she ever did find a daddy for Dillon, it would have to be a man who really wanted to be a father. Someone who'd always hoped and planned to be a father. And from what Laramie had told her, he didn't fall into that bracket.

Deciding she'd spent enough time with the man, she began to gather up the dishes and carry them over to the cabinet. She was scraping the leftovers into a plastic bowl when he came up behind her.

"Don't do that. I'll take care of it."

His low voice was like water flowing over a bed of gravel. Just the sound of it caused her eyes to close and goose bumps to cover her forearms.

"This is my job," she said thickly. "Not yours."

"Not tonight."

The lowly spoken words caused her to spin around, and as soon as she was facing him his arms slipped past her waist until his hands were planted on the counter's edge. The move pinned her in a seductive trap between him and the cabinets.

With her heart pounding, she dared to glance up at him. "What are you doing?" she asked.

One corner of his mouth lifted to a vague smile. "I'm trying to apologize."

Her mind leaped backward as she tried to recall what he'd said or done that had been so offensive.

"Apologize?"

"For asking you to heat my supper. I'm a big boy who can take care of himself." Lifting both hands to her face, he rubbed both thumbs against her cheekbones. "But I wanted an excuse to have your company."

She had to force herself to breathe. "Laramie—that doesn't make sense," she finally managed to say.

"You're right. A grown man like me shouldn't be playing games. I should've just asked you to join me. But I was afraid you'd turn me down. Instead I used your job to get you in here."

She should push his hands away, she thought. She should duck her head under his arm and scurry out of the room. But something about the touch of his hands, the gentleness in his eyes made her want to be close to him.

"I'm nothing special," she murmured.

"I happen to think you are."

The thickness in her throat was very close to becoming a ball of tears. And as she blinked her eyes to ward away the moisture, she wondered how different her life might have been if she'd met Laramie three years ago. Probably no different at all, she told herself. She'd only been seventeen at the time. He wouldn't have looked at her as a woman back then. And now, well, it felt as though she'd grown a decade older.

"I'll be leaving the ranch in a little while. So we can only be friends."

His blue gaze locked on to hers. "I have friends who

happen to be women. But I don't want to touch their hair or hold them in my arms or kiss their lips. The way I want to do with you."

It was one thing to be courted by a brash guy who hadn't yet learned to be a man. But it was quite another to have a mature, responsible man like Laramie imply he was attracted to her.

"There must be a shortage of women here on the ranch," she tried to joke.

"It takes a special breed to live on this ranch and like it. And I haven't exactly been looking for a woman." His hands left her face to flatten against the small of her back. "But I've been looking at you."

His touch activated every cell in her body, yet his words affected her the most. It would be so easy to let herself hold on to this rugged man, to let his strength comfort her, his sexuality pleasure her. But she didn't want to make a fool of herself a second time. She had Dillon to think of first.

"Laramie, I'm still not over Heath," she said bluntly.

His brows pulled together. "Heath? Was that Dillon's father?"

Just hearing that name connected to the word *father* was laughable. Heath had been a joke, she thought, a very sad joke.

Looking away from him, she said bitterly, "Only in a genetic sense. He's the furthest thing from a parent that anyone could be."

"Are you still in love with him?"

His question momentarily stunned her, but then she suddenly realized that Laramie didn't know what had happened between her and Heath. He had no way of knowing that the guy had killed her love with his deception. "No! Our relationship ended when he walked out."

"Love doesn't always end just because that person hurts

you. And I have no idea of how you once felt about the man. You must have loved him. Otherwise, I don't think you would've had his baby."

Groaning with embarrassment, she moved out of his arms and walked out to the atrium. There the footlights running along the pathway to the house cast a faint glow of light across the plants and cushioned wicker couch, but Leyla was too restless to sit. Instead she stood staring out at the lawn, remembering the evening Laramie had joined Dillon on the swing set. The image of the two of them together had touched her in a way that she'd not fully understood until now.

She was still standing by the glass wall when she heard Laramie's footsteps enter the atrium, but she didn't look around, even as his hand came down on her shoulder and her insides wilted at his touch.

"You shouldn't be embarrassed for being human, Leyla," he said quietly.

She tried to swallow away the thickness in her throat. "I was too young to know the man was using me, Laramie. At the time…I thought I loved him. I believed everything that he told me about the two of us getting married and having a home and family."

"I figure you wanted to believe him. That you needed to believe him."

The fact that he understood that much gave her the courage to turn and face him. "I guess I was looking for love and security. You see, things at home were never that great. My dad always talked about work, but he never did much of it. Mom cleaned houses in town to pay the bills. From what my sisters tell me it's still that way with my parents."

"And you wanted something better for yourself."

She sighed. "Don't get me wrong, Laramie. A higher standard of living wasn't what I was looking for when I met Heath. I'd never had much. And a person can't really know about that sort of stuff until they're exposed to it. What I wanted was to feel safe and protected by someone who cared about me."

"You didn't get that from your parents? Your siblings?"

"Dad only loves himself. And Mom only has so much to spread among us four kids. My sisters and I care about each other. But they were always jealous of me—because people called me pretty and not them. It's hard to say about my brother. He's very quiet and pretty much keeps to himself."

His fingers kneaded her shoulder. "So Heath made you feel loved and wanted."

She nodded ruefully. "Until I told him about the baby. Then he turned into a complete stranger. At first he accused me of trying to trap him, and then he accused me of sleeping around. Finally he admitted he was the father but that he'd never had serious intentions toward me. He'd said he didn't want any part of raising a kid or paying child support. That crushed me. But I realized I didn't want a guy like him around me or my baby."

"What did you think about having the baby?"

"At first I was frightened because I knew my father would be angry. It turned out that he was so furious he more or less drove me out of the house and away from the family. But that made my pregnancy even more special to me. The coming baby meant that I would have someone who needed and loved me."

"That's all behind you now," he said softly.

"Yes, I've put Heath far behind me. But I still question every little step I take. And I hate being that way. I wish I could just let myself live and quit worrying that I'm going to be one of those women who makes the same bad choices over and over."

His hand moved into her hair and her breathing grew

shallow as he gently stroked his fingers through the long strands. His touch made her feel so special, more special than she'd ever felt in her life.

"You don't have to second-guess yourself now, Leyla. You made the right choice to come here to the ranch," he said quietly. "And I promise you, I'm not going to be deceptive or mean to you."

With everything inside her, she wanted to believe him. Yet she couldn't begin to know what was really in this man's heart. And until she found out, she could never risk hers.

Closing her eyes, she said, "It's easy to make promises, Laramie. Keeping them is the hard part."

"I'm smart enough to know I'll have to earn your trust, with more than words."

She'd not been expecting anything like that from him, and before she could stop herself she turned and rested her cheek against the middle of his chest.

His hands settled lightly against her back as though to say she could stay or go. The choice was hers to make. The fact that he was giving her that choice gave her the courage to linger and let the comfort of his embrace wash over her.

The atrium was so quiet she could hear the steady beat of his heart and for a few precious moments, she let the sound lull her, the warmth of his body spread into hers. But all too soon that warmth stirred desire deep within her and with a sense of regret, she eased back from him.

"It's getting late. I'd better go check on Dillon," she told him.

"Good night, Leyla."

"Yes. Good night," she murmured, then hurried into the house before her body could persuade her to run back to him.

* * *

The next morning at breakfast, Leyla didn't see Laramie. Whether he'd been called out on some ranching matter or had still been asleep, she had no way of knowing. She wasn't about to climb the stairs and check his room, and she told herself not to fret about the man. It was Sunday, anyway, and she wasn't expected to cook his meals today.

Sometimes she asked herself if she actually had a job. If it weren't for cooking meals for her and Dillon and making lunches and snacks for Sassy, she wouldn't have much to do at all. At least the idle time was giving her the opportunity to dig into the textbooks on nursing Bridget had given her.

Thankfully, when she'd left the family home and gone to live with Oneida, she'd been able to finish the last semester of high school on the reservation and receive her diploma. Now she had plans to attend college and become a nurse so that she could help people just like her aunt. Maybe that was too lofty a dream for a young woman raising a child on her own, but she was determined to reach her goal.

Later that morning, she was changing linens on Dillon's bed when she heard a faint knocking noise out in the small living area.

Expecting to find her son banging his toys together, she was surprised to see he was busy with his crayons and coloring book.

"Dillon, what was that noise? Were you pounding on something?"

"No." He shook his head and pointed to the door that separated their apartment from the main house. "That noise there."

As Leyla started toward the door, the knock sounded again, making her hurry across the thick carpet. When she opened it to find Laramie standing on the threshold, her mouth very nearly fell open. Even though he basically lived in the same house, he'd never come to her door or implied he wanted to visit her apartment.

"Laramie," she said, trying not to stare at the rugged image framed by the doorway. Everything about him spelled the word *man* in big bold letters.

This morning he was wearing his usual cowboy work gear of jeans and boots and black cowboy hat, except that his sturdy denim shirt had been replaced with a moss-green cotton. The sleeves were rolled up to expose his forearms, and the color made the blue in his eyes stand out even more. But it was the lazy curve of his grin that made her heart do a fluttery two-step.

"Good morning," he said. "I was beginning to think you and Dillon must still be asleep."

"At eleven o'clock?" She laughed outright. "That would be the day."

"Uh—" He peeped past the partially opened door. "Are you busy?"

Realizing she was treating him like an unwanted salesman, she pushed the door wide and motioned for him to enter the apartment. "Please come in. I was cleaning in the bedroom and didn't hear your knock. And I've warned Dillon not to open the door for anyone. I guess I should explain to him that here on the ranch it's okay."

He said, "He's learned a good rule. No need to confuse him by breaking it now."

At that moment, Dillon looked up from his coloring book and spotted Laramie standing next to his mother. The child leaped to his feet and raced over to join them.

Squatting to Dillon's level, Laramie gathered him in the circle of his arm. "How's my partner today?"

"You not eat breakfast," the boy said with a faint pout.

Faintly surprised, Laramie glanced up at Leyla. "I didn't realize he kept tabs on me."

"He watches for you," Leyla explained. *And so do I,* she could have added.

Laramie's attention turned back to Dillon. "I'm sorry that I missed breakfast with you, Dillon. Did you eat what your mommy made for you?"

The boy gave him one affirmative nod. "I ate it all up."

"That's good. That means your muscles are going to grow fast." He made a show of testing Dillon's upper arm. "Think you're strong enough to ride a pony today?"

"Laramie!" Leyla practically gasped. "I don't—"

Dillon's dark brown eyes popped wide open. "Yeah, yeah! Ride pony! I wanna ride pony!"

Leyla rolled her eyes while Dillon jumped up and down with excitement.

Laramie smiled at her. "Trust me, Mommy, it will be fine. You'll see."

I'll have to earn your trust. When he'd spoken those words to her last night, something in his voice caused her to melt inside. And from that moment on, she'd realized it would be wrong to shut him out without giving him the chance to prove himself trustworthy.

"If you're sure about this," she conceded. "Dillon has never been up close to a large animal like a horse or cow."

"Well, he's about to do both," he said with a grin. "You two get ready and we'll walk down to the barns."

She glanced at a digital clock sitting on a nearby table. It was already after eleven. "What about lunch? Wouldn't it be better if we waited until after we ate?"

"I already have lunch for the three of us planned." He clapped his hands in a hurry-up gesture. "So get with it, woman. Time is wasting."

Questions whirled through her mind, but she didn't

voice them. Dillon was already bouncing on his toes with excitement, and to be honest with herself, she was excited, too. Last night she'd told Laramie that she wished she could simply let herself live and enjoy. Well, today she was going to try to do just that.

"Come on, Dillon," she said while reaching for her son's hand. "If you want to ride the pony, you'll have to put on your jeans. Cowboys wears jeans. Right, Laramie?"

"You bet," he said, the grin returning to his face. "And cowboys never cry, either."

Pausing she glanced around at him. "Never?" she asked skeptically.

"Well, almost never," he amended with a shrug.

She couldn't imagine this strong, rugged man ever shedding a tear. But he'd been Dillon's age once. Had he cried for a mother who was nowhere to be found? He couldn't have, she thought. At Dillon's age, he'd not even known what having a mother meant. Just like Dillon didn't know what it was to have a daddy. But later her son would grow up to learn exactly what he was missing. What would she tell him then? What had Laramie's old guardian told him?

Whenever I look at Dillon I see a lot of myself.

Laramie's telling words had set Leyla's mind to thinking and her heart to aching. But she was going to do her best not to dwell on those poignant thoughts today.

"That's good to know," she told Laramie. "The next time Dillon has a crying fit, I'll be happy to let you deal with him."

Chuckling, Laramie gave the boy a conspiring wink. "I have all kinds of things to cure crying fits."

"That's what scares me," Leyla said with a good-natured groan, then hurriedly ushered her son into the bedroom.

Chapter Six

The sky was practically clear and the sun already very warm when, a few minutes later, the three of them left the house and started walking in a westerly direction toward the barns.

As they traveled along at a slow pace, Dillon held on to Laramie's hand and made a game of jumping over every rock that was larger than the size of an egg. Next to them Leyla enjoyed the sun on her face and the tangy scent of juniper and pine drifting on the breeze. May was a beautiful time in New Mexico, particularly when she could be outdoors sharing it with Laramie and Dillon.

It was Sunday so the work had been geared down to only taking care of necessary chores around the barn. Even so, a group of saddled horses was tethered outside a wooden corral and two men were loading bales of alfalfa onto a flatbed truck.

As the trio walked past, the men acknowledged them

with a wave. Leyla figured they were probably surprised to see Laramie with a woman and child in tow. From what Sassy had told her, he wasn't seen around the ranch with women. Did that make her special? No. Laramie was only being kind to a child who desperately needed a man's company. That was all this was about, she told herself.

They'd walked a fair distance from the house when Dillon's short legs began to slow. Laramie stopped and looked down at him. "Have you ever been on a piggyback ride, Dillon?"

Dillon looked puzzled and Leyla explained, "He doesn't know what you mean."

After slanting her a meaningful look, he bent down to the boy. "Okay, Dillon. Climb onto my back and put your arms around my neck, then hold on tight. Really tight."

The boy did as he commanded and once Laramie raised to his full height, he took a firm hold on Dillon's little legs.

"Look, Mommy! I'm high up! Real high!" Dillon shouted with a happy squeal.

Leyla smiled up at her son. Thanks to Laramie, the child's eyes were sparkling and it was plain to see he was on the adventure of his life. "Yes, you're way taller than I am now," she said to him.

Traveling the next hundred yards at a faster pace, they finally reached the area where Laramie had left a saddled pony inside a small wooden corral.

Laramie lowered Dillon to the ground and led him over to the board fence. "Dillon, this pretty pony's name is Cocoa. And he especially likes boys like you. Want to take a closer look at him?"

Dillon nodded without hesitation, and Laramie lifted the boy so he could peer over the top rail of the fence. Laramie called to the pony and the animal immediately came trotting over to inspect his visitors.

Dillon watched in awe as Laramie stroked the horse's blazed face.

"You can touch his nose, too," Laramie encouraged the boy. "Cocoa likes to be patted. He's a big baby."

Dillon tentatively reached out and touched the white stripe on Cocoa's face, then looked at his mother and giggled. "He's a baby pony, Mommy. See? He likes me."

"The baby pony has big teeth," Leyla couldn't help saying.

Laramie laughed. "The better to eat you with, my dear," he teased Leyla, then quickly added, "Don't worry. Cocoa doesn't bite or kick or buck or have any of those nasty habits. He's one of the horses that Riley and Clancy ride when they're here visiting the ranch. Cocoa is what we cowboys call bombproof."

Leyla sighed with relief. "That's good to know."

For the next few minutes, Laramie allowed the child to get acquainted with the horse before he finally took him into the corral and lifted him into the tiny saddle.

Once he was actually on Cocoa's back and Laramie had secured his feet in the stirrups, Dillon was beside himself with excitement, yet to Leyla's surprise he obediently followed Laramie's instructions to sit still and not yell or flap his legs.

"Grab on to this and hang on tight. Just like you held on to my neck," Laramie told the boy as he guided Dillon's little hands to the saddle horn. "And here we go."

Laramie began to lead the pony in a very slow walk around the corral. As Leyla watched the two of them, she couldn't stop a rush of emotion from misting her eyes. Her son was riding a horse for the very first time in his life. And all because Laramie had cared enough to give Dillon the time and attention. No matter what happened between her and the ranch manager in the future, Leyla would always be grateful to him for this.

She called to Dillon from her perch on the fence, saying, "You look like a real cowboy."

Laramie stopped the horse alongside the fence where she sat. "Dillon will really look the part when he gets a pair of boots and a hat," he told her.

Leyla had to stifle a groan. Didn't the man realize Dillon was listening to every word? The child would hound her for days now about boots and a hat.

She'd not even gotten the thought out of her head when Dillon spoke up, "Me want boots and hat, Mommy. Like Laramie."

She shot Laramie a reproving look. "Now look what you've done. Those things are far beyond my budget. Why did you—"

Laramie lifted a hand to interrupt. "Before you get all bent out of shape, let me deal with this. Most likely Riley and Clancy have plenty of stuff they've outgrown. I'll ask Maura if she has anything stored away that might fit Dillon."

Leyla had never met Maura Cantrell, but she did know that the woman was Dr. Bridget Chino's sister and that the two women worked together at Dr. Chino's medical clinic in Ruidoso. Leyla would be forever grateful to Bridget and her husband, Johnny—not only for helping deliver her son, but also for being her friends and helping her get this better-paying job at the Chaparral.

"Well, if Maura is anything like her sister she must be a very kind lady. But I wouldn't feel good about you imposing on her."

He shot her an impatient look. "There you go again. Remember what I told you about everyone helping each other around here?"

"Yes. But that's not good unless it goes both ways. It's not right for me to always be on the receiving end. And I don't know of anything I could do to help a woman like Maura Cantrell."

"Just be a good employee and a friend. That's enough, Leyla. You don't need money to do that."

"Boots. I gonna wear boots and hat." Dillon emphasized the last statement by plopping the palms of his hands atop his dark brown hair. "I gonna be cowboy."

The happiness on her son's face made everything else seem insignificant, and she smiled at him. "Okay, if you're going to be a cowboy, what is Mommy going to be?"

Tilting his head to one side, Dillon contemplated her question for a moment. "You gonna be Mommy."

"Smart kid," Laramie said with a laugh.

After several more minutes of Dillon riding the pony, Laramie suggested it was time they stop for lunch. Because cowboys had to eat and stay strong, he explained to Dillon. But the riding instruction continued as he showed the child how the horse had to be taken care of by removing his bridle and saddle and brushing down his coat.

"Cocoa is hungry," Dillon told Laramie as the two of the walked out of the corral.

"I'm sure he would agree with you," Laramie said with a chuckle. "But it's not time for him to eat yet. It would give him a belly ache if he ate too much."

"Me no belly ache," Dillon said, then rubbed a hand across his tummy. "Me hungry."

"I am, too, partner."

After giving Leyla a hand down from the fence, he ushered the two of them over to a white pickup truck. After the three of them had climbed into the dusty cab, Leyla asked, "Where are we going? Back to the house to eat lunch?"

"Not the house," Laramie answered. "You and Dillon see plenty of that place. I have our lunch in the back of the truck in an insulated chest. The bunkhouse cook threw some things together for us."

Since she'd come to work on the ranch, the only people she'd met other than Laramie were Quint, Sassy and Reena. She had a natural curiosity about the crew that worked with Laramie, especially because she never heard him say a bad word about any of them. "That was very thoughtful of the cook. Especially since it's Sunday."

"Ernesto is a good guy. Doing for others makes him happy."

"Have you known him for a long time?"

Laramie started the engine and backed the truck away from the corral fence. "He was here on the ranch for a couple of years before I came."

His remark took her by surprise. "You've lived here on the ranch for that long?"

"Nearly eighteen years."

As he set the truck in forward motion, she glanced across the bench seat at him. "You must have been very young when you moved here. What about the man who raised you? Didn't you want to stay with him until you reached adulthood?"

"Diego had diabetes in the worst kind of way. When his health began to really fail, he made me promise that once he died I would come here to the Chaparral and speak to Lewis about work. I was sixteen when Diego passed on. Just a kid, more or less. Lewis, that was Quint's father, was still alive back then. And I was fortunate that he took me under his wing. He gave me a job and a place to stay in the bunkhouse."

Trying to picture Laramie at that young, vulnerable

age, she asked, "Did you know how to do ranch work back then?"

"Quite a bit. Diego had always had cattle and horses and goats. He'd taught me how to care for them and handle myself around livestock. So it wasn't like I was a greenhorn. I had lots to learn, though. And over the years, I have."

Many times in the past Leyla had felt ignored and forsaken by her family. And when she was really having a pity party for herself, it felt like she didn't have a family at all. Yet being estranged from her family was far different than not having any family at all. If she really wanted to see her folks, she could swallow her pride and go back to Farmington and stand up to her father. Laramie didn't have even that option and that reality bothered her greatly.

"So as a teenager you must have really taken to this place," she said.

"At first I missed Diego something awful. Besides that, the other ranch hands were quite a bit older than me, and that made me feel out of place. But they were all kind enough to put up with a wet-nosed kid and after a while it started feeling like home. Now, it is home."

"Do you ever get the urge to leave?" she asked. "To build a place of your own?"

He frowned. "Why should I do that when I'm perfectly happy here?"

There was a testy note in his voice, one that told Leyla he didn't appreciate her question. She didn't let it deter her, though. Not when Laramie didn't think twice about plying her with personal questions.

"Because you don't own this place," she answered. "It belongs to someone else. You work very hard and you're so devoted to your job. Seems like you'd want your efforts to benefit you."

"Is that what's important to you? Owning things?"

"A home isn't just a 'thing,'" she said defensively.

He slanted her an annoyed look. "Well, my home is here. I don't care about the name on the deed."

The man was satisfied with what he was and where he was. And that was well and good for him, Leyla thought. As a teenager he'd lost his father and his home. He deserved to be happy and contented now. She only wished that her and Dillon's future was as settled as Laramie's and that once they left this ranch they would have a decent home waiting for them.

"It's nice that you feel so deeply about this ranch. Everyone needs a place where they feel like they belong," she said quietly.

He turned his head slightly to look at her, and this time she could see that his features had softened.

"Maybe you and Dillon belong here, too."

His subtle suggestion set her heart to pounding, and she purposely turned her gaze away from him and out to the passing landscape.

"Only for a while," she murmured and wondered why those words put an ache in her heart.

For the next ten minutes Laramie drove the truck on a westerly dirt track that took them away from the ranch yard and close to the river's edge. Along the way, Laramie remained quiet and preoccupied and Leyla got the impression that he was disappointed in her for some reason.

Maybe he'd not appreciated her question about him leaving the Chaparral to build a ranch of his own. Or maybe he'd expected her to say more about her future plans. She didn't know what the man was thinking and she tried to tell herself it didn't matter. But that would be a lie. Laramie was beginning to matter to her. Very much.

"Cow, Mommy! Cow!"

Dillon's excited shouts pulled Leyla out of her thoughts and turned her gaze toward the windshield. Her son had spotted a large herd of red cattle with white faces.

"Yes, I see. The cows are eating grass." She responded to her son, then glanced at Laramie. "I've only seen black cows at the ranch yard. These are different."

"They're Herefords. Normally we only run Angus, but we decided to invest in a couple hundred of these just to see how they play out on the cattle market. After we eat, I'll take Dillon for a closer look," he told her."

"I'm sure he'll like that," she murmured.

A short distance on down the road, the hard-packed dirt track split in two directions. Laramie took the one that climbed a short distance up a foothill covered with juniper and piñon pine. When they reached the top of the incline, Leyla let out a gasp of delight.

"Oh, how beautiful!"

Below them, the river valley stretched for miles. To their right a ridge of tall pine-covered mountains stood sentinel over the herds of grazing cattle.

"I thought you and Dillon might enjoy eating here," Laramie spoke up. "It's a pretty view and there's plenty of open space here for Dillon to safely explore."

"It's great, Laramie," she said. His thoughtfulness left her feeling somewhat awkward. She'd never had anyone go to this much trouble to give her and her son an enjoyable outing, and she could only wonder if he was expecting something from her in return.

No, she mentally argued. He wasn't the sort of man who expected payment for doing a thoughtful deed. She needed to quit worrying about his motives and simply focus on enjoying this special time with Laramie and Dillon.

After parking the truck, Laramie lifted the chest with their lunch out of the back of the truck and carried it over to a flat area sheltered on one side by a stand of juniper. Two fallen logs had created a natural L shape perfect for seating.

"Looks like someone has built fires up here before," Leyla commented as she spotted a ring of blackened rocks.

"Me and a few of the guys stop here sometimes and brew a pot of coffee. It's a nice place to rest before we finish the ride to the ranch yard."

The ranch yard was a good five or six miles away from this spot, she calculated. She couldn't imagine herself staying in the saddle for that long, but when she looked at Laramie's tough, sinewy body, it was clear he had the stamina to keep going far beyond a normal person's endurance.

To Leyla's utter surprise, the bunkhouse cook had gone to the trouble of cooking them a meal of fried chicken and the usual picnic additions to go with it. Dillon ate everything she placed on his paper plate, then asked for more.

Once his tummy was finally full, the boy wandered a few steps away to dig in the dirt with a stick. As Laramie watched him form a shallow trench and fill it with tiny pebbles, he said, "I believe Dillon is enjoying all of this, don't you?"

On the smooth, bleached-out log, Laramie was sitting no more than a hand's width away from Leyla and as she turned her face toward his, the distance between them seemed even closer. His nearness caused her pulse to skitter and her breathing to quicken.

"Very much. Other than me taking him to the park, no one has ever bothered to take him on a picnic before. You're giving him all sorts of new adventures."

A faint smile grooved his cheeks and Leyla couldn't help thinking that for such a rugged man, his blue eyes looked so soft and tender, so very tempting.

"What about you? Have you ever been on a picnic before?"

"My sisters and I used to have play picnics in the backyard. We'd pretend we were in a big city park with lots of people in fancy clothes strolling around. And we'd have wonderful things to eat, like exotic fruit that we'd never even seen, much less eaten." She let out a wistful sigh. "But that was when we were little girls. We didn't understand what being poor really meant. It's funny how I look back on those times now and think of us as being rich. At least, us being all together made it feel that way. But it will never be like it was when we were little girls pretending to have a picnic."

Reaching over, he slipped his big hand over hers. "Nothing stays the same, Leyla. Children grow up. Some day Dillon will be a man and he'll strike out on his own—away from you."

"Maybe that's why my mother stays with my father," Leyla replied on a pensive note. "She doesn't want to be alone when all of her children are gone."

"No one wants to be alone," he said.

The warmth of his hand and the soft, husky sound in his voice pulled at her, and she couldn't stop her gaze from settling on his lips or her memory from reliving his kiss.

"Laramie, when I talked to you earlier about building a ranch of your own, it wasn't my intention to offend you." The urge to touch him was so great, she couldn't stop herself from laying her hand on his forearm. "I was… I guess I'm just curious as to why a man as gifted as you doesn't strike out on his own."

Something flickered in his eyes before his gaze dropped to her hand resting on his arm. "Someday I'll try to explain everything better—why this ranch means so much to me."

"Is living here the reason you've not married?" she asked.

That brought his eyes back up to hers. This time there were shadows in the blue depths.

"Partly. It's hard to get interested in a woman when right off the bat she wants to change me—move me away from all the things I love. I used to tell myself there had to be a woman out there somewhere who'd take me as I am and be happy to live on this isolated ranch. But I gave up looking."

"You said partly. What's the other reason you haven't wanted to marry?"

His gaze flickered back to hers and Leyla's breath caught in her throat. She'd expected to see defiance in his eyes, not a lost and hungry look that made her want to wrap her arms around him and hold him close to her heart.

"Like I told you, Diego was an old bachelor. It was a long time before I ever knew what a husband was, and even then it was just a word to a kid. I went from a bachelor's home to living in a bunkhouse with a bunch of other bachelors. Lewis was a husband, but I never saw him interacting with his wife, Frankie. I guess I learned more about what it means to be a husband after Quint married Maura. And that was just a few years ago."

"So you didn't grow up with a role model," she stated.

"That exactly what I'm saying."

She shook her head. "I thought maybe you weren't married because you'd had your heart broken or something like that."

His lips twisted to a wry line. "A few little breaks. Nothing like what you went through."

Her gaze swung to Dillon. "Having a child changed my life and I don't regret it. Dillon is my life. Just like the ranch is yours."

And she'd be crazy to think they could all blend together. She wanted a home for Dillon and herself. She wanted permanence and security. She wasn't yearning for riches, or things or a fancy house. She only wanted a home. One that couldn't be taken away from her.

Suddenly it dawned on her that her hand was still resting on Laramie's arm and his hand hadn't moved from hers. Being close to him felt almost natural. But where was all of this going to take her? she wondered. Straight to another heartbreak?

The thought had her easing away from him and rising to her feet.

"I think we'd better show Dillon the cows, then start back. He takes a nap in the late afternoon. He'll be getting sleepy pretty soon."

"Sure," he said. "Let's walk down this side of the hill. There should be a herd right below us."

By the time Laramie drove the truck through the ranch yard, shadows were extending out from the barns and adjoining corrals. The ranch hands were spreading feed to the penned livestock and Dillon had fallen asleep with his head resting against his mother's arm.

After Laramie parked the truck at the backyard gate and killed the engine, he looked across the seat at her. "Will he wake if I carry him?"

"He'll never know it," she assured him. "I'll walk ahead and open the doors for you."

As soon as Laramie scooped the child up, he understood what Leyla meant. Dillon's little arms and legs were limp as he cradled the boy against his chest and started toward the house.

Inside Leyla's apartment, she motioned him into a small bedroom furnished with two twin beds. He placed the sleeping child on the one that she pointed to, then watched as she removed his tennis shoes and placed them on the floor.

"He's really out of it," Laramie said with amazement. "I didn't know that kids could sleep so soundly."

"I'm sure all the fresh air and excitement did him in. He'll be up early. But that's okay. He had such fun today."

She covered Dillon with a light blanket, then turned from the bed. "What about you?" Laramie asked. "Did you have fun?"

"I enjoyed it very much," she told him, then gestured toward the open door of the bedroom. "Would you like to have some coffee or something? Or do you need to get down to the barns before the day ends?"

"I need to check on my mare. The one that had surgery. But I'll do that before I go to bed. Right now coffee sounds good."

They walked into the living area and Leyla motioned for him to take a seat, but he shook his head. "While you fix the coffee, I'll go to the truck and get the leftovers from our lunch. There's a container of brownies in there, remember?"

She smiled at him. "Yes, I remember you have a sweet tooth."

And she had very sweet lips, Laramie thought. That was something he couldn't forget. Even now the urge to pull her into his arms and kiss her was rolling over and over in his mind. Yet sweet as it would be to kiss her again, he didn't want to risk ruining the day or the closeness he could feel growing between them.

But was getting close to the woman what he really wanted and needed? What would he do if by some miracle Leyla actually fell in love with him or he fell in love with her? Ask her to marry him? Hell, he didn't know how to be a husband. He'd already made that clear to her.

And she was far too precious to hurt with a dead-end affair. But he wanted her. Not just physically. He wanted her company, wanted to hear her voice, see her smile, drink in the sultry scent of her hair and body and pretend, yes pretend, that she would always be with him.

"Laramie? Have you changed your mind about the coffee?"

Her voice penetrated his thoughts and he realized she was waiting for him to follow her out the door and into the main house.

"Changed my mind? Not at all. Let's go."

Ten minutes later they were sitting in the atrium drinking coffee and finishing the brownies when Laramie pointed out the splendid sunset spreading across the western skyline.

Leyla set aside her cup and walked over to the end of the room where the glass wall faced the ranch yard.

"How beautiful," she murmured. "Everything is pink and gold and lavender."

Laramie came up behind her and placed a hand on the back of her shoulder. "It is beautiful," he agreed. "The whole day has been pretty special to me. I figure you may have enjoyed a trip into town more, but Dillon seemed to like being outdoors with the animals."

"Dillon loved it and so did I."

She turned slightly and the movement caused his fingers to catch in her hair. He used the opportunity to lift a silky strand to his nose and draw in its subtle scent.

"Where do you get the idea that I'm a town girl?" she asked. "I've never lived in town."

"I thought you lived in Farmington before you moved to your aunt's place on the reservation," he said.

"My parent's house is a few miles from Farmington.

It's on the same property where my paternal grandparents lived before they passed on."

"Hmm. I've not done much traveling, but I've been through that area. It's mostly high desert plains with lots of cliffs and rock formations. What did you do there for fun?" he asked.

She shrugged. "Sometimes my sisters and I would go to town and see a movie or window-shop at the mall. But we only had enough money to do that occasionally. I played on a softball team until I was sixteen. And I used to hunt for Native American artifacts with friends. Lots of Indian ruins are located in that area. I've saved pieces of pots and tools that I've found so that when Dillon gets older I can show him and teach him about his heritage."

That didn't surprise him. She had a pride about her that he admired. "Did you work when you still lived at home?"

She nodded. "At night, after school. I bussed tables at a steakhouse in town. I had my driver's license then but no car, so my mom or sister would pick me up after work. Until I—" Her lips pressed into a thin line and she looked away from him.

"Until you what? Met Heath?"

Surprised, she turned and stared at him. "How did you know I was about to say that?"

He shrugged. "Just a feeling. It's a cinch you had to meet the guy somewhere. Must have been the steakhouse."

"No. I wished it had been. Then I probably wouldn't have given his flirtation any notice. But he was a friend of my cousin, Alonzo. They worked together as roughnecks in the oilfields. He was a twenty-two-year-old charmer, and I thought because he was such a good friend to Alonzo that he would be trustworthy. By the time I realized he wasn't, it was too late. I'd already gotten too deep into his lies."

He touched the back of his forefinger to the faint dent

in her chin. "Leyla, when I think of what that bastard did to you I'd like to hunt him down and beat him until he needs his jaw wired shut." He shook his head with disgust. "Guys like him aren't men. They're worse than creatures that crawl on their bellies in the dirt."

She sighed. "You don't think he was simply being a man, taking what he wanted?"

"Hell no! Didn't your mother teach you that a man should treat you with respect? Diego was never a husband, but he knew right from wrong and he taught me that much. And that a man had to stand up to his responsibilities."

She dropped her head. "I'm not sure my mother knows how a man should treat her. All she knows about is men like my father." Lifting her head, she gazed up at him. "Heath did turn out to be a scummy person. But in the end I was the stupid one, Laramie, for allowing myself to get involved with him. And I never intend to be stupid again."

With his hands on her shoulders, Laramie drew her to him. As she settled her cheek against the middle of his chest, the fierce need to love and protect her left an aching knot in his throat.

"You've grown into a woman since then, Leyla. You need to trust yourself just as much as—well, as much as you need to trust me."

"I'm trying, Laramie," she said, her voice muffled by the folds of his shirt.

For most of Laramie's youth, he'd been shy and awkward around the opposite sex. Later, his encounters with women had mostly been the short, casual kind where genuine affection in any form hadn't been required. So he was hardly a practiced lover. But with Leyla everything felt natural, not clumsy or contrived. When he touched her it was actually an extension of the feelings in his heart. And that stunned him.

Drawing her closer, he bent his head and pressed a kiss to the top of her shiny black hair.

"I'd better go," he said wistfully. "I've got some things I need to deal with before morning. We'll be leaving before daylight, so I won't be around for breakfast."

Easing her head away from his chest, she frowned. "Leaving?"

"Roundup. Remember?"

"Oh. I'd forgotten."

The disappointment on her face made him nearly giddy. "We'll be starting on the far western boundary of the ranch and that's several miles away. So I won't be back for a couple of days or more."

Her gaze locked on to his. "I'm going to miss you."

With a helpless groan, he closed the space between their lips. And though he was ravenous for the taste of her, he kept his kiss thorough but brief. Otherwise, he couldn't have stopped with just one or two. He wouldn't have wanted to stop until they were making love.

Easing away from her, he reached for his hat and started toward the door. "I'll miss you, too, Leyla. Please explain to Dillon why I'm not around."

"I will. Goodbye," she said.

At the door he gave her a little wave, then hurried down the steps before he could let the lost look on her face persuade him to stay.

Chapter Seven

Laramie had been away from the ranch for two days, and Leyla had stayed busy by helping Sassy tend a vegetable garden she was growing on a spot not far from the ranch house. Once the vegetables were ready to be harvested, Sassy had plans to donate them to some of the hungry and needy people in the area. Leyla had also used some of the leisure time to study. But this afternoon Dillon was growing impatient with being inside. For the past ten minutes he'd poked and prodded and whined to get her attention.

"Me wanna see Cocoa, Mommy. Wanna see Cocoa," he repeated while earnestly patting her knee.

Deciding they both needed a break, Leyla put her book aside and drew her son into a tight hug.

"You want to see Cocoa, do you? Well, I suppose the two of us could walk down to the barns and find him. Think you can walk beside Mommy for all that way?"

Jumping out of her arms, Dillon hopped around the coffee table on both feet. "I can. I can. And we can see Lar-mee, too. Okay, Mommy?"

Leyla sighed. "No, Dillon. I told you, Laramie is gone right now. He's working—roping cows, giving them a shot and writing a name on their hip."

Dillon quickly picked up a crayon. "Write. I can write name."

"Yes, you're learning to write," Leyla agreed. "But Laramie is doing a different kind of writing. He'll tell you all about it later."

"Find him, Mommy. Let's find Larmee."

She was missing the man, too, so she understood how Dillon was feeling.

"We can't find him. He's out in the mountains and too far for us to go. But we'll go find Cocoa and give him a carrot to eat," she promised.

After exchanging Dillon's shorts and tennis shoes for a pair of jeans and sturdy shoes, they left the house and started toward the barns. This time without Laramie to carry her son partway, the trek took much longer.

When they finally reached the corral where Dillon had ridden the pony, the animal was nowhere to be seen. The crestfallen look on her son's face was a sign of just how much her son had taken to the ranch and all the things it had to offer a boy.

"Don't worry. Cocoa will be around here somewhere," she told her son.

"Miss, can I help you?"

At the sound of the man's voice, Leyla turned around to see an older man wearing a gray, sweat-stained Stetson and leather work gloves. From the looks of him, he had to be a ranch hand. Laramie had implied that everyone would be away from the ranch working roundup, but she supposed this man had been left behind with a skeletal crew to take care of barn chores.

"Hello," she greeted him. "I'm Leyla, the cook who's filling in for Reena. And this is my son, Dillon. We were looking for Cocoa—the pony that belongs to the Cantrell boys."

The older man smiled broadly. "Well, nice to meet you, Leyla and Dillon. I'm Saul. I can take you right to Cocoa. He's over in a paddock with a few other horses. Follow me and I'll show you."

Saul led them behind another big barn where a large paddock covered several acres of grassy area. As they approached the tall board fence, Leyla spotted the brown pony grazing with four other horses.

Saul said, "I can halter him and bring him over to the fence. That way your little guy can see him up close and give him that carrot."

Apparently this man was as connected to the pony as Laramie. He'd simply called to the horse and Cocoa had come running. But even a novice like her could see that Laramie had a special affinity with animals. With her, too, she thought with resignation. So far her plans to keep her distance from the ranch manager had been a dismal failure.

"That's too much trouble," she told Saul.

"No trouble at all," he assured her. "You two just wait right here."

Minutes later, a happy Dillon was standing on the fence, stroking Cocoa's nose and chattering to the horse as though the animal could understand every word.

A few steps away Saul said, "I'd heard that Reena had gone over to Apache Wells. That was bad luck about Jim breaking his leg like that. Just goes to show you that you can't trust those damned stallions."

Leyla looked at him. "Jim broke his leg while he was riding?"

"Oh, no. He was leading the animal when it reared up and knocked him to the ground. From what Abe said, the horse pounded on old Jim pretty good."

The image sent chills over Leyla. Laramie worked with horses every day. Was he facing that kind of danger?

"That's awful."

"Yeah, but it could have been worse. At least Jim will recover." The ranch hand tossed a speculative glance her way. "I was surprised to hear that Quint had hired a new cook. I figured Frankie would come home to take over."

Frankie was Quint's mother and from what Leyla understood, the woman spent most of her time these days in Texas with her two older sons from an earlier marriage.

"I don't think Laramie would want Mrs. Cantrell making such a sacrifice just for him," Leyla carefully commented.

He shrugged and grinned. "Naw. I guess not. And the Cantrells have money to burn, you know. They could hire a dozen cooks and not ever see a dent in their bank accounts."

Leyla was wondering if this man resented the Cantrell's wealth when he suddenly spoke again as though he'd read her mind.

"Don't get me wrong. The Cantrells being rich is a good thing. Not a family in these parts deserves it more than them."

Not knowing exactly how to reply to this man's gossip, she said, "I'm grateful to be working for them."

"I am, too," he said with a grin, then added, "and I'd better get back to my chores. I'll go ahead and take the halter off Cocoa, but don't worry, he'll hang around as long as the boy is giving him attention."

She thanked him and after he'd dealt with the pony's halter, the man took off in the direction of the barn.

Leyla joined her son on the fence, and after giving Dillon several more minutes with the little horse, she suggested to him that they let Cocoa get back to eating grass and they would go look at more animals.

Thankfully, Dillon agreed and they walked deep into the ranch yard, which was surrounded on both sides by numerous buildings and mazes of corrals. Several of them held small herds of yearling calves, and the two of them had paused to look at the cattle when a tall woman dressed in jeans, rugged cowboy boots and a loose chambray shirt emerged from a nearby building. Her long chestnut hair was tied back with a yellow-and-blue scarf. As she grew closer, Leyla could see that she was very pretty. She was also pregnant.

"Well, hello," she called as she made her way across the cattle pen.

"Hello," Leyla said once the woman was in speaking distance. "My son and I were just looking. I hope we're not bothering anything."

"Not at all." She pulled off her glove and stuck her hand through the fence. "I'm Laurel Hollister. My husband is the resident vet here on the ranch. I'm his assistant."

"And I'm the new cook." Leyla shook the other woman's hand. "Laramie has spoken of you and your husband. It's always with great admiration, too."

Laurel laughed. "That's good to know."

The woman focused her gaze on Dillon, who'd turned his attention away from the cattle to cast the tall woman a wary eye.

"I must look pretty scary to him with all this dirt and manure and blood on me," she said with another laugh.

"I've been sewing up a goat that got in a fight with a wire fence. She wasn't too happy until I finally got her sedated."

"You take care of that sort of stuff instead of your husband?" Leyla asked curiously.

"Not usually. But I can handle some things when he's not around. Right now Russ is gone with the rest of the crew on roundup. I stayed behind to take care of any problems that might arise here." She smiled and patted her rounded tummy. "And Russ didn't think it would be too good for me to sleep on the ground."

"Not too comfortable, either," Leyla added with a knowing smile.

Laurel let herself out of the cattle pen and walked over to where Leyla and Dillon stood beside the fence. For the next few moments she took great pains to introduce herself to the child.

"He's adorable," she said to Leyla. "You must be very proud of him."

Leyla nodded. "Dillon is a blessing. When is your baby due?"

"October. So, God willing, we'll have our son or daughter to celebrate our first Christmas together as a family."

Christmas as a family. Since Oneida had gone into the nursing home, it had just been she and Dillon together for the holidays. And sadly, she couldn't imagine that changing unless her aunt was fortunate enough to be released from the nursing facility by December.

"You don't know whether it's a boy or girl?" Leyla asked.

"Russ and I want to be surprised. Not knowing the sex just adds to the excitement."

Yes, it was easy to see that this woman was very excited about her coming baby, and Leyla wondered how it would feel to be pregnant with a child that was loved and wanted by his father. How would it feel to know that a man would be at her side through the pain and the joy? She'd missed so much when she'd been pregnant with Dillon. She'd loved and wanted her baby, but the uncertainty of her future and the feelings of abandonment had taken away most of the special joy. And now she wasn't sure she'd ever have the courage to trust a man enough to have his child.

"I wish you good luck."

"Thanks." Smiling warmly, Laurel gestured toward another big building to their left. "Want to come stroll through the barn where we keep most of our patients?"

"It's nice of you to ask," Leyla told her.

"I'm not being nice—I'm being selfish," Laurel confessed. "It's not often that I get to visit with another woman."

Leyla said, "Sassy has been telling me how nice you are and I've been wanting to meet you. I'm planning on becoming a nurse and that's what you do."

Laurel chuckled. "Yeah, I guess you could call me an animal nurse. So we have something in common to talk about—taking care of animals and people." She placed a warm hand on Leyla's shoulder. "Come on and I'll show you some of my patients."

Inside the building, the three of them passed through a nicely furnished office where Laurel introduced them to an older man named Maccoy. Behind that room, they passed several treatment areas before they eventually reached a boarding section where stalls and pens lined both walls.

Leyla was amazed to see everything from cows, calves and horses, to goats, a dog and even a mother cat that had decided she wanted to give birth in an animal hospital. As for Dillon, he was enthralled with all the animals, especially the cat.

He gazed, transfixed at the yellow queen and her

brood of yellow-and-white kittens nestled in a bed of hay. "Tommy, Mommy. That's Tommy."

Leyla glanced ruefully at the other woman. "Tommy was a cat we had to give away before we came here. He misses him."

"Awww. Well, we can easily fix that," Laurel told her. "We've had several litters of kittens here at the barns born this spring. Dillon can pick out the one he likes and take it back to the house with him. Actually, you should let him pick two. They do better if they have a brother or sister for company."

Leyla's immediate thought was to politely refuse the woman's offer, but suddenly the memory of Laramie's words drifted through her mind.

We all treat each other like family around here. And Dillon needs to learn to be a part of it.

Laramie was right, she realized. And she needed to start thinking about the things she and Dillon *could* do instead of the things they couldn't. "Thanks. We might do that later."

Just accepting the woman's offer made her feel incredibly good, and for the next few minutes she found herself talking and laughing more than she had in a long time.

When she finally announced to Laurel that she and Dillon needed to start back to the house, the woman quickly offered to drive them, but Leyla declined the offer, saying she and Dillon both needed the exercise.

As they walked toward the house Dillon chattered continually about the animals they'd seen in the vet barn. Especially the cat and kittens.

"Tommy has babies. He licks their heads."

Leyla chuckled to herself. "That wasn't Tommy," Leyla tried to explain. "That was a mommy cat. And she was licking the babies' heads to clean them. Like I clean your face with a washcloth."

Dillon's little features wrinkled into a frown as he suddenly paused and stomped both feet. "That's Tommy! He come here. We need to get him and take him with us!"

She didn't know why Dillon was being so stubborn and argumentative about the cat. Perhaps giving up Tommy had affected him more than she'd realized. Or was all of this crankiness stemming from Laramie's absence these past few days? If her son had asked about the man one time, he'd asked a hundred.

Squatting down to her son's level, she gently gathered his hands with hers to garner his attention. "You aren't being a nice boy right now. And—"

Her words trailed off as a truck suddenly rolled to a stop a few steps away from them. Leyla glanced up from Dillon's mutinous face to see Laramie climbing out of the truck cab. The sight of him sent happiness rushing through her and she quickly turned Dillon around so that he could see the man walking up behind him.

"Look who's come home," she told him.

"Larmee! Larmee!" Dillon cried as he raced straight to Laramie's outstretched arms.

As Leyla watched him swing her son up into his arms, joy poured into her heart like a beam of pure sunlight. He truly cared about Dillon and that meant everything to her.

Smiling, Leyla walked over to them. "Hello," she greeted.

"What's going on with you two? Are you lost?" Laramie teased.

The sparkle in his eyes sent her heart into a rapid thump. "We came to see Cocoa," Leyla explained. "Saul helped us find his paddock, so Dillon got to visit with the pony."

"That's good. I'll have to thank Saul for that."

"We see Tommy," Dillon chimed in. "And he had babies. Mommy said it wasn't Tommy. But it was."

Laramie gave Leyla a wink, then said to Dillon, "Well, I'll just have to take a look at this cat. But right now I'm going to take you and Mommy on a little trip. Wanna go?"

Forgetting all about Tommy, the child shouted, "Yeah! Yeah!"

"What kind of trip?" Leyla wanted to know.

With a hand at her back, Laramie ushered her to his truck. "I'm taking you and Dillon to dinner. A special kind of dinner—chuck wagon style."

At the big house, Laramie waited while Leyla changed her skirt and blouse for jeans and a T-shirt. And because he'd warned they would be out after dark and the mountain air would grow cool, she gathered jackets for Dillon and herself.

Once they climbed back into the truck, Laramie set their course in a westerly direction. This time, he took a trail that closely skirted a ridge of tall mountains.

Nearly forty minutes after they left the ranch yard, the truck forded a shallow creek then climbed to an open meadow. At one side was a copse of aspen trees. The chuck wagon had been set up there, and nearby a campfire was already burning. Not far from the camp, beneath the shelter of the trees, at least twenty horses were tied to a long picket line.

Dillon noticed the animals first and eagerly pointed to them. "Horses! I see horses!"

"That's right, partner," Laramie told the boy. "We'll take you for a close up look at them while Ernesto finishes cooking dinner."

He parked the truck a short distance away from the camp, and as he helped her to the ground, she said, "This looks like a scene right out of a Western movie. When you said the ranch still does roundup the traditional way, you really meant it."

"Down through the years, we've changed the way we do some things on the ranch, but not this one," he said proudly.

Once they reached the campsite, Laramie introduced her and Dillon to Ernesto and then to the rest of the crew. Now that the workday had ended, several of the men were milling about the campfire, while others sat on seats they'd fashioned from fallen logs and overturned feed buckets. The group of cowboys ranged from young to old and came in all shapes and sizes.

Normally, Leyla wasn't comfortable with crowds and she'd definitely never been in a group of men as the only woman present. But they all greeted her in kind, gentlemanly fashion and in no time she felt completely comfortable and even welcomed.

After Leyla and Laramie exchanged a few words with the men, he suggested they take Dillon for a look at the horses before it became too dark.

"These horses aren't ponies like Cocoa," Laramie told the boy as they approached the picket line. "Sometimes they stomp and kick. So you'd better let me carry you."

"I wanna walk," Dillon protested. "I'm big."

He started to dart off in a run, but Laramie snagged the child before he could get two steps away.

Swinging him up into his arms, Laramie said firmly, "Big boys can get hurt, too. So if you want to see the horses, you have to do what I tell you."

Dillon seemed to realize that Laramie meant business and immediately settled comfortably in the crook of his arm. At the picket line, the three of them strolled slowly down the row of horses. Among the herd, Laramie sought out the ones that wouldn't attempt to take a bite out of the boy's little hand and allowed the child to stroke their noses. After Dillon had patted the last one, Laramie suggested it was time to return to the campfire.

This time Leyla was completely amazed when her son unexpectedly burst into tears and tried to wriggle out of Laramie's arms.

As they strode back to the campground, Laramie asked the boy, "Now what is this? Remember how I told you that cowboys don't cry? Well, you're a cowboy, aren't you?"

Sniffing hard, Dillon nodded, then buried his face against Laramie's neck. The emotional display took Laramie by surprise, and he cast Leyla a puzzled look.

Sighing, Leyla shook her head. "I'm sorry, Laramie. I don't know what's gotten into him today. I think—well, I think he's been missing you. I tried to explain why you weren't around, but I think he's been angry because you left."

"Oh," Laramie said softly. "I'm sorry he's missed me that much."

Leyla smiled faintly. "I've missed you, too."

He cast her a teasing glance. "You're not going to cry, too, are you?"

Her eyes twinkled as she continued to smile at him. "No. I only cry at movies."

"Well," said Laramie, "then I might have to take you one day. And bring along some tissues." And he grinned back at her.

After a supper of steaks cooked over the open fire, barbequed beans and sourdough biscuits, Ernesto pulled out a sack of marshmallows.

Laramie roasted several marshmallows for Dillon, and having never experienced the gooey sweet before, the little boy couldn't get enough. But after too many to count,

Leyla suggested to Laramie that he stop before the boy developed a stomachache.

As the fire burned down and talk around the camp grew quiet, one of the men pulled out a guitar and began to softly strum a lilting melody. Eventually, the food and the long busy day got to Dillon, and he fell asleep on Laramie's lap.

"Ernesto has a cot in the chuck wagon," Laramie suggested. "If you'd like to stay a bit longer I could put Dillon in there where he'd be comfortable."

"As much as I'm enjoying the evening, I'd better take him home before it gets too late," she told him. "Would you mind?"

"Of course not. I hadn't planned on keeping you out late anyway."

After Leyla had thanked Ernesto for the delicious meal and said goodbye to the cowboys, they started the long drive back to the ranch house. Between them in the booster seat, Dillon slept soundly, while Leyla was content to gaze out the windshield and recount the day.

"I'm sorry Dillon wasn't on his best behavior this evening," she said after they'd traveled several minutes in silence.

"Dillon was fine."

"I don't like for him to cry and whine."

"He's a little boy. And I hate that my being away from the house has affected him."

"He has to learn that people can't always be around just because he wants them to be."

Pushing his hat back on his head, he rubbed a hand across his forehead. "You're tough."

A wan smile touched her lips. "That's better than being hurt."

"Yeah. I guess most anything is better than being hurt."

He glanced over at her. "Did you mean what you said earlier? About you missing me?"

His question brought a blush to her cheeks. "I did mean it," she said huskily. "See, I'm as bad as Dillon."

"It's nice to be missed, Leyla. Very nice."

By the time they arrived back at the ranch Laramie's boots should have been dragging with exhaustion. Instead he felt like he was walking on a cloud. Having Leyla and Dillon with him at the campsite tonight had been more special to him than he could have imagined.

Throughout the evening she'd asked him all sorts of questions about the roundup in general and the jobs of the cowboys and their horses. She'd seemed genuinely interested, which lifted his spirits higher than high. No matter how much he told himself he didn't want a wife, he kept dreaming of the three of them as a family, of even giving Dillon a brother or sister.

Dreaming couldn't hurt anything, he told himself. Until he began to want all those dreams to come true. That's when the hurt might come. But tonight he wasn't going to dwell on that thought. Tonight he wanted to show Leyla exactly how much he'd missed her.

Inside the house, he carried Dillon to the same bed that he'd placed him on the other evening. Laramie stood to one side while Leyla dealt with his shoes and clothing, then pulled the cover up to his chin.

"He's probably dreaming about horses," Leyla said as they left the bedroom.

Unable to ignore the need in him any longer, Laramie snared an arm around her waist and tugged her close against him. "And I'm dreaming about you," he murmured.

"Laramie."

His name was whispered softly, like an evocative plea that pulled on every masculine cell in his body.

"I've had a hell of a time working when all I can think about is kissing you," he spoke against her lips. "Holding you close to me."

Moaning softly, she rose up on her toes and slipped her arms around his neck. "Then maybe you'd better kiss me," she murmured.

The invitation had him closing his eyes and fastening his lips over hers. This time the sweet familiarity of her taste was like coming home after a long, hard ride. The pleasure was a mixture of relief and triumph.

As his lips searched hers, he could feel her body stretching and straining against his, the mounds of her breasts pushing into his chest. Her willing response shot thrills of heat through his body and an ache deep in his loins.

He kept the kiss going until the need for oxygen finally forced them apart. But Laramie wasn't content to let the embrace end. He swiftly scooped her up in his arms and carried her over to a long couch on the opposite side of the room.

Once he'd sat with Leyla comfortably cradled in his lap, she gently protested.

"Laramie, I'm too heavy for this."

The low chuckle in his throat was a sound of pure desire. "You're as light as a feather," he murmured. "But maybe you need to stretch out after that long ride."

Placing her on the cushions, he immediately leaned over her until their faces were mere inches apart.

"Is that better?" he asked huskily.

To answer his question she pulled him down beside her and pressed her lips to his. Her clear signal sent Laramie's senses reeling and as he deepened the kiss, his hands automatically began to explore her soft curves.

It wasn't until his fingers found their way beneath the hem of her T-shirt and began stroking her soft skin that she shifted away in protest.

"Laramie—I—I'm sorry," she said in a tight, stricken voice.

Frowning, he sat up and raked a hand through his mussed hair. "Leyla, I don't want to do anything that makes you uncomfortable. If that—"

Quickly, she scrambled to a sitting position and gathered one of his hands between hers. "It's not you, Laramie. I'm—" With an anguished groan, she looked away from him. "I need to tell you that I've not let any man touch me like that since—"

"Dillon's father," he finished flatly.

"Yes. And I guess it sort of scares me. I want you to touch and kiss me. Very much. But then my mind starts whirling with all those bad memories and I feel myself falling into a dark, scary pit."

Gently, he gathered her chin between his thumb and forefinger and pulled her face back around to his. "I understand, Leyla. I've had a few of those scary pits myself. You just need time. Remember that I'll always be around to catch you and keep you from falling into those dark places."

Closing her eyes, she rested her cheek against his strong arm. "Not always. Eventually Reena will come back and my job here will be over."

Did that mean everything between them would be over, too? he wondered. His brain refused to consider the idea.

"What do you plan to do then?"

Sighing, she lifted her head away from him, then slowly rose to her feet. "I've been saving all the money I can to start nursing school. I can get grants to help me, but I'll still need extra money to make up for the working hours I'll have to give up."

Surprised by her revelation, he asked, "What makes you want to be a nurse?"

She moved away from him and the couch and began to amble around the small living room. "Several things. My aunt Oneida for one. I see how much it means to an ailing person to have someone care for them, even in the smallest way. And when Bridget delivered my baby under such harrowing conditions, I was amazed. And the more I thought about it, the more I wanted to be in the medical field so I could help people in the same way."

"Those are admiral reasons. I'm just not sure—well, you've told me that you're tough. But I don't see you that way. The suffering you'd see in the medical field might squash your soft heart."

She glanced over her shoulder at him and as Laramie's gaze slipped over the long black hair, the tiny waist and flared hips, he wished he had the right to carry her to bed and show her that loving him wasn't dangerous.

"In other words, you don't believe I'm emotionally strong enough for the job." She shook her head. "I might be afraid to have sex and fall in love. But the notion of nursing sick people doesn't daunt me." She turned her gaze to the darkened window. "And with a nursing job, I can buy a home of our own. One that no one can take away from us."

After thinking about her words for only a few moments, he rose from the couch and walked over to where she stood. "I have a feeling you could make your home right here if you wanted to. Quint would be happy to—"

"I don't want handouts," she interrupted.

"Believe me, Quint expects anyone he hires to work. It wouldn't be a handout."

Shaking her head, she said, "Call me independent if you want, Laramie, but I want a house and property of my own. Something worthwhile to pass on to my son. Right now that's my main goal in life. It's what keeps pushing me forward."

"So you think those material things will make you happy? I don't think so, Leyla."

Twisting around so that she was facing him head on, Leyla stared in amazement at him. "Laramie, you more than anyone should know how it feels to suddenly be thrust on your own. After Diego died you probably felt homeless—until you settled here. Am I so wrong in wanting a home for myself?"

"A home, no. A house and property, that's something different. You need to stop and realize that a home can be anywhere as long as you're with the people you love."

Bending her head, she muttered, "At one time I had that with my family back in Farmington. Then I was pushed away and had to move in with Oneida. But by the time I started to feel as though my aunt really loved me and that I belonged with her, she suffered the stroke. I just feel like—" Her throat was suddenly so tight she had to stop and swallow. "I need something solid in my life, Laramie."

Stepping closer, he laid his hand on her shoulder. "I understand how you feel, Leyla. Like you can't depend on anyone but yourself. But this notion that a house will fix things—it isn't right."

Confusion flickered in her dark brown eyes and then with a torn cry, she flung her arms around his waist and buried her face against his chest. "I don't want you to think badly of me, Laramie."

Her anguished plea was muffled by his shirt. As Laramie held her close, something like love was filling up the empty space in his heart.

"I don't think badly of you, Leyla. I just think you have your wants and your needs mixed up."

And he probably did, too, he thought. But it was too late to do anything about that now. The need for a home was pushing her forward. Well, the need to have her in his life was pushing him forward and it wasn't going to stop until he finally had her.

Chapter Eight

By the time Laramie and his crew finished the spring roundup and returned to the ranch, Dillon's birthday had come and gone. Laramie felt badly about missing the boy's important milestone. Especially after learning that no one but his mother and Sassy had been around to help the child celebrate.

Laramie had passed many a birthday without anyone around except Diego and he wanted things to be better for Dillon. Not that there was anything wrong with Diego. The old rancher had been a good man and a wonderful mentor to him, but Laramie had missed the softness a mother would have brought to his life. Yes, Dillon was missing out on a father's touch, but at least when little Dillon grew to be a man he would know the woman who'd given birth to him. That was something Laramie would trade all the birthday parties in the world for.

Steering his truck through the busy Ruidoso traffic,

Laramie darted a glance at the two boxes lying on the passenger seat. He'd paid the store clerk extra to have the items gift wrapped. Back at the ranch there was a pile of work waiting for his attention, but he'd not let any of it deter him from driving to town and buying Dillon a belated birthday gift.

The idea had Laramie mentally shaking his head. Finding a woman he could truly care about was something he'd given up on a long time ago. And he'd surely never pictured himself falling for a woman with a child. Hell, he was the furthest thing from a father that any man could be. But Dillon had become important to him. Along with his mother. Now he was asking himself just how deep he was willing to let his feelings keep growing.

Since the night she'd talked about her plans to become a nurse and buy a place of her own Laramie had been trying to tell himself he needed to put a whoa on his feelings for the woman. Jim wasn't going to wear a cast on his leg forever. Soon Leyla and Dillon would be moving on and he'd be left alone. Laramie wasn't a dreamer. He realized it was senseless to invest his heart in a relationship that couldn't last. But his heart and his body refused to listen to logic. He wanted to be near Leyla, to touch and hold her, make love to her. Even more, he wanted to make her dreams and wishes come true.

If that meant that he'd already fallen in love with her, then he was in trouble. Unless he could somehow make her see that living on the Chaparral with him could be the home she was searching for.

That evening, Laramie purposely waited until after the three of them had eaten supper before he presented the gift boxes to Dillon.

"These are for you, Dillon. Happy Birthday, partner," he said to the boy.

Wide-eyed, Dillon stared at the boxes sitting in the middle of the kitchen table, then quickly shook his head back and forth.

"Not today," the child argued. "My birthday gone."

Laramie tossed Leyla a rueful look. "He's smart enough to know he doesn't have a birthday every day." Bending at the waist so that his face was on level with Dillon's, he said to the child, "I know your birthday was three days ago. I wanted to be here then. But I couldn't be. So I'm giving you gifts now. Okay?"

Dillon studied him for long moments, then touched a finger to one of the boxes. "Mine?"

Laramie chuckled. "Yes, those are yours. So tear right into them."

Dillon looked to his mother for guidance and when Leyla nodded her permission, he quickly dove into the box sitting nearest to him.

While the boy ripped into the paper, Leyla shot a sidelong look at Laramie. "You shouldn't have gone to so much trouble. Taking us to the chuck wagon supper was enough of a treat for Dillon. He's still talking about that night."

"I'm glad he enjoyed it. But that was more of a treat for me." Smiling slyly, he inclined his head toward the boxes. "These things are just for Dillon."

Four days had passed since he and the men had finished their work on the range, and during that time he'd been working overtime. Most nights he'd come in very late to find his supper in the warming drawer on the range and the lights in Leyla's apartment already off. As a result he'd seen her and Dillon only a few minutes at breakfast. Coming into a dark, empty house had reminded him just how attached he'd become to Leyla and her son. And how much he'd miss them if they weren't in his life.

"It was very kind of you to celebrate his birthday with gifts," she said.

While Dillon tugged at the last of the paper, Laramie edged closer to Leyla's side. "I've been missing you," he admitted in a low voice.

Her gaze remained on her son, but he could see her throat working as she swallowed.

"You've been leaving early and coming in late."

"We're still trying to catch up on everything that was left undone while roundup was going on. Plus, the last couple of evenings I've had to meet with Quint and discuss some ranching matters that couldn't be done over the phone. It's a long drive over to the Golden Spur."

She glanced his way. "Mr. Cantrell didn't want to come here to talk? Because he owns the Chaparral, I'd think he'd want to look things over for himself."

"Quint and I are like brothers. He trusts me. He doesn't need to see things for himself, unless he just wants to. And right now Maura is expecting their third child, so he doesn't like heading off at night and leaving her alone with the boys. That's why I make the drive."

"Oh. I didn't know his wife was pregnant. If that's the case, then Mr. Cantrell is clearly a thoughtful man. And so are you," she added huskily. "And—"

"Boots! Mommy, look! I got boots!"

Leyla stepped toward her son and the little cowboy boot he was holding up for her to see. Made of black leather, the tall shaft had intricate inlays of red and white that shaped the form of a thunderbird. "Oh, my. Those are—" Her words trailed away as she glanced over her shoulder at Laramie. "The boots are too much."

Laramie chuckled. "Pretty bright, aren't they? But we cowboys like to show off—just a bit."

"That's not what I meant." She shook her head with dismay. "The cost. I—"

"I wanna wear them, Mommy. Can I?"

Before she could answer, Dillon plopped down on the chair and jerked off his tennis shoes.

Laramie chuckled. "I think he likes them, Mommy. Let's just hope they fit. I snuck a look at his tennis shoes for the size. Boots fit differently, though, so I tried to make a close guess."

Impatient with the adults, Dillon began to kick his feet. With a hopeless smile, Leyla knelt to help him. Once they had the boots in place, the boy immediately jumped down from the chair and awkwardly clomped across the kitchen tile.

"Looks like you made a perfect guess on the size," she told Laramie.

The grin on his face deepened as he watched Dillon strutting around the room. "Cute, aren't they?"

She turned slightly toward him and the tender smile on her face made him feel ten feet tall. "Very cute. Thank you, Laramie. For giving him something so special."

The desperate urge to touch her had him curling his arm around the back of her shoulders. The soft warmth of her body filled him with the need to be closer. "Believe me, Leyla, it's just as much fun for me to give to Dillon. And I want—" His words halted as he took his gaze off Dillon's boot hopping to gaze down at her face. "I want things to be different for Dillon than they were for me."

A curious frown pulled her brows together. "I got the impression that you had a happy childhood with Diego."

To Laramie's amazement, he felt his throat tighten with emotions. "I did. I guess seeing you raising Dillon alone has reminded me of all the things I missed. He cared for me but never let me forget he wasn't my real father." He let out a long breath. "Back then I didn't know I was missing anything. The naïveté of a child is a blessing, I guess."

Her dark eyes softened as they swept over his face and Laramie wondered if she'd been thinking about him these past few days, if she'd come to the realization that he wasn't going to hurt her.

"Yes. I suppose you're right," she murmured.

His gaze lingered on hers until the need to kiss her became so strong it was too uncomfortable to bear. Turning his attention to Dillon, he watched the child jump and stomp his way across the kitchen floor.

"Leyla, do you think Sassy would watch Dillon for a couple of hours tomorrow afternoon? I'd like to take you somewhere away from the ranch."

"Dillon can't come with us?" she asked with a heavy dose of skepticism.

"He could. But I'd rather it just be the two of us. There's something I want to show you." He turned his gaze back to her and spotted all sorts of doubts dancing across her face. "It's important to me or I wouldn't ask, Leyla."

Her expression thoughtful, she glanced over at Dillon. "If it's important to you, then I suppose I can go. After all you've done for Dillon I owe you that much."

With both hands on her shoulders, he turned her to face him. "You don't *owe* me anything. If you agree to go with me, I'd like for it to be because you want to. Not because you feel obligated."

He watched her closely as all sorts of questions and doubts flickered in her eyes. "Leyla," he said softly. "I promise this is not some sort of hidden agenda to get you alone. After we talked the other night I…well, I think you need to know some things about me. That's all."

A faint smile slowly appeared on her face. "All right. If Sassy doesn't mind watching Dillon, I'll be happy to go."

He breathed a sigh of relief. "Great. If everything is going smoothly here on the ranch, let's plan to leave about one. That way we'll get back by Sassy's quitting time."

"That sounds good."

Feeling like a grinning fool, he jerked his head back toward the package on the table that was still unopened. "I think Dillon's so taken with the boots he's forgotten he has another gift to open."

"I expect he'll want to wear the boots to bed. I'm almost afraid to see what's in this next box," she teased, then called to her son.

The cowboy hat that Laramie had purchased to go along with the boots was also black. The brim was laced around the edge with leather and was equipped with a stampede string to keep the cowboy gear firmly attached to Dillon's head.

The child was just as excited with the second gift as he was with the first. While Laramie and Leyla sat at the kitchen table with coffee and dessert, Dillon was content to race an imaginary steed around the kitchen and through the long adjoining hallway.

But it wasn't long until all the excitement wore him down and he climbed onto Laramie's lap. With his little head nestled comfortably against Laramie's chest, he was on the verge of falling asleep when Laramie's cell phone went off and startled the drowsy child.

Leyla quickly pulled her son over to her lap so that Laramie could get to the phone. As soon as he spotted the number on the ID, he knew he couldn't let the call go to voice mail.

After a brief exchange of words with Seth, the manager of the calving operation, he reluctantly rose to his feet.

"I've got to go. There's been some trouble with a fence up on the north range. Some Chaparral calves have gotten over on Tyler Pickens's land. It's the last thing we need to happen around here."

Leyla looked at him with concern. "Oh. You say that like the man might cause trouble."

Laramie screwed his hat down low on his forehead. "He's a bit of a hothead. I'm not expecting to have trouble out of him, but I have to go tend to all of this." At the door, he cast her a look of regret. "Good night, Leyla."

"Good night, Laramie," she returned. "And please be careful."

"I plan to," he said wryly, then hurriedly stepped through the door.

The next day, after helping Sassy in the garden, Leyla was dressed and waiting on the back patio when Laramie finally returned to the ranch house. She'd not seen him since he'd left last night, and she was about to think he'd forgotten their date.

It's not a date, Leyla. The man simply wants to show you something that is important to him. It's not like he's taking you out to a candlelit dinner.

She knew the voice in her head was right, but the thought of being totally alone with Laramie filled her with all kinds of anticipation.

"Is that a couple of kittens I see peeping out of that little dog house?" Laramie asked, as he approached her. "Dillon was telling me about them last night."

He was dressed in all denim and from the saddle stains she spotted on the legs of his jeans, he looked as though he'd been working on horseback.

"It is. Laurel helped us pick them out and I let Dillon name them. The girl is Cookie and the boy is Stripes."

"Very original for a boy his age," Laramie said with a grin.

"I gave him a few suggestions," she confessed. "When they get old enough Russ is going to spay and neuter them for us. That way when we leave the ranch and take them with us, we won't have to worry about them reproducing."

The smile fell from his face. "So you still have leaving on your mind?"

"It's not something I'm dwelling on," she lied. "It's just a reality." A fact that she had to face, she told herself. If she was ever going to get her nursing degree and that home for herself and Dillon, she would have to leave the Chaparral.

Ever since the night of the chuck wagon supper she'd been trying to convince herself that when it was time for her to leave the ranch it wouldn't be painful to walk away from Laramie and move on with her life. But she knew she was lying to herself. That night in the atrium when he'd held her so gently and she'd confessed her fears of being intimate with him, something had changed in her. Sharing that part of herself with Laramie had been like stripping off her clothes and allowing him to see her completely naked. In an odd way she felt closer to him now than ever. And she was also realizing more and more just how much her body and her heart hungered for him.

Standing a step or two away from her, he said, "That's one of the reasons I want to take you on this little trip today."

His remark intrigued her, but she decided not to press him to explain. She didn't like talking about the future. Not now. Now that he'd come into her life and clouded all her bright plans with uncertainty.

Glancing at him, she offered, "I'm ready to go if you are. I've already said goodbye to Dillon. Sassy is playing a game with him. She'll keep him happy while we're gone."

He glanced down at himself. "I should probably change clothes—I smell like a horse—but I don't want to take the time."

Smiling faintly, she reached for her handbag lying in the seat of a lawn chair. "I like the smell of horses."

A chuckle rumbled in his throat as he reached for her arm. "Why, Leyla Chee, I didn't know you could flirt."

Her cheeks felt more than warm as he began to lead her across the yard to his waiting truck.

"That wasn't flirting," she corrected. "Just stating a fact."

"Well, either way, it's good to know the smell of me won't bother you," he said.

Oh, it would bother her all right, she thought. Everything about him bothered her, stirred her up in ways she was trying not to think about. For nearly four years now she hadn't allowed a man to even touch her. Now she was willingly going off with Laramie to some place she didn't even know.

You're forgetting every hard lesson you learned, Leyla. You're letting yourself forget every heartache that Heath ever caused you. That's what you're doing.

Leyla's troubled thoughts must have shown on her face. As they drove away from the ranch house, Laramie asked, "Is something wrong?"

Realizing she was gripping the armrest, she moved her hand to her lap and tried to make herself relax. "No. Why do you ask?"

"Because you look like I'm driving you to an execution or something."

Shrugging, she did her best to smile. "Sorry. It's just that ever since I've come to work here at the ranch, I've not had to leave Dillon for any reason."

"It will be good for him to be away from his mother for a little while. Good for you, too," he added.

"You're right. Eventually I'll have to get used to him going back to a daycare facility."

His pointed glance made Leyla shift uncomfortably in the seat.

"Dillon is your whole life, isn't he?"

"He's everything to me," she conceded.

He reached across the console for her hand and as his fingers wrapped around hers, Leyla's heart beat hard and fast.

"I'd like to think you have a little room in your life for me, too," he said lowly. "Or is that asking too much?"

Sighing, she looked away from him and out the window. "I don't know, Laramie. When I first came to the ranch, I wasn't planning on meeting someone like you."

"I never thought I'd meet anyone like you," he gently countered.

She turned her head to see a faint smile carving a dimple in the side of his cheek and his dark, sexy profile pulled at every womanly cell in her body.

He went on, "It's awful that Jim had to break his leg in order for us to meet."

She smiled. "I worked at the Blue Mesa for nearly a year before coming here. Several of the Donovans eat there regularly and Mr. Cantrell sometimes. But I don't recall ever seeing you while I was on duty."

His hand left hers to return to the steering wheel, and Leyla felt a pent-up breath ease from her lungs.

"I don't go into town unless it's necessary. And while I'm there I usually don't have time to sit and linger over lunch. Something on the ranch is always needing my attention."

Smiling now, she said, "The ranch is your whole life, isn't it?"

He looked at her and grinned. "It always has been. But believe me, Leyla, I can make room for you and Dillon, too."

Afraid to reply to that, she turned her gaze back to the passing landscape. By now they'd reached the long wooden bridge that crossed a narrow portion of the Rio Bonito. Beyond it they would pass through several more miles of Cantrell land before reaching the main highway. The drive through the river bottom was exceptionally pretty, with willows and aspens interspersed with rugged piñon pine. Wildflowers dotted the meadows, while sagebrush bloomed along the edges of the dirt road. Here and there black Angus could be seen grazing on the summer grass. The idea that everything before her eyes belonged to one family was difficult for her to imagine.

It was the sort of wealth she'd never aspire to have. All she'd ever wanted was a decent home with sturdy walls, a solid roof and dependable plumbing. A house where she and her son would be warm and sheltered and never have to worry about being pushed out by the owners.

Suddenly aware of the long moments of silence ticking between them, she asked, "Will you tell me where we're going now?"

"To my place."

His place? That night in the atrium he'd mentioned having a house and land, but that was all. He'd certainly not said anything to imply the property was that important to him. She looked at him with confusion. "I don't understand. I thought—"

"I'll explain when we get there," he interrupted.

Seeing he didn't want to discuss the subject now, she turned her gaze back to the countryside and tried to assure herself that agreeing to be alone with Laramie for the next couple of hours wasn't a mistake. After all, she was a grown woman now. Not a teenager who could be seduced by the first man to give her a second glance or a line of lies. And Laramie was far, far from Heath's sort. She had to remember that and hope that she wasn't making a fool of herself a second time.

Chapter Nine

Once they were on the highway, they traveled at least ten more miles before Laramie steered the truck onto a graveled road. Leyla looked around with interest as they passed through low rolling hills covered with blooming sagebrush and snags of twisted juniper trees. Green grass and pastel-colored wildflowers nodded in the bright afternoon sun.

"This is very pretty," Leyla remarked. "Is this your land we're going over now?"

He pointed to a section of sturdy H braces and strands of barbed wire stretched tight against fat cedar posts. "My land starts right up there at the next cross fence."

"How much acreage do you own?"

"Two hundred acres. It's enough to carry a few mama cows and their calves."

She looked at him with surprise. "Oh. I didn't realize you had cattle of your own."

"The subject never came up," he said, then gave her a

brief smile. "Besides, I don't want to bore you with too much cattle talk."

"You're so busy on the Chaparral. When do you have time to take care of these cattle?" she asked.

"Right now while the grazing is plentiful, the herd doesn't need much attention. But I have a man hired to keep a close watch to make sure all is well—especially when they're calving. During the winter he takes care of the everyday feeding, too."

Laramie slowed the truck, then turned left onto a steep, graveled driveway. At the bottom of the hill sat a small stucco house with wooden shingles on the roof and thick board shutters on the windows. Though small, the structure appeared to be freshly painted and in perfect condition.

As they drew closer, Leyla leaned forward for a better look. "This house belongs to you, too?"

"It does. The remainder of the property runs eastward, behind the house." He cut the engine and unsnapped his seat belt. "Come on. I'll show you around."

He came around to her side of the truck and helped her down to the ground. As his hand lingered on her elbow, she lifted her gaze to his and suddenly she felt as though she'd just been shaken awake from a long sleep. Everything around her looked different. Especially him. After Heath had turned her world upside down, she'd done her best to keep herself and Dillon shuttered away from the world. And in doing so she'd not really opened her eyes to the lives of people around her, to the joys and pains they were going through.

"Laramie, before you show me around, I—I want to apologize."

Surprise arched his brows. "For what?"

Her expression rueful, she glanced past his arm to the

huge cottonwood shading one end of the house. "For assuming that you only wanted to work for the Chaparral instead of wanting a place of your own. You should have told me about this piece of land—that you raised cattle for yourself."

His eyes narrowed. "That makes a difference in how you feel about me?"

Seeing that he'd misconstrued her, she frowned at him. "Not the way you're thinking."

"How am I thinking?"

Glancing away from him, she swallowed. "That I'm all about acquiring things and wealth. That I believe everyone should have those same ambitions. Including you. But that's not right. All I've ever wanted is a measure of security. To have somewhere to belong."

His eyes suddenly softened and her heart melted as he touched his fingertips to her cheek. "When I had to leave this place, that was all I wanted, too. Just to know I would be in a place where I'd always be safe and warm and fed."

A long breath eased from her. At least he understand that much, she thought with relief. "Yes, that's exactly how I feel."

Placing a hand on her shoulder, he urged her toward the small yard surrounding the house. A mixture of grass and weeds covered the loamy soil; a few patches of prickly pear popped up here and there. Other than the massive cottonwood that shaded the north side of the structure, there were three aspens behind the house. As the two of them strolled along in silence, Leyla couldn't help but wonder if there'd ever been a woman on this homestead. One who planted flowers and vegetables, raised children and dreamed of growing old with the man she loved.

Laramie interrupted her thoughts. "This was my home until I was nearly sixteen."

Stunned by this revelation, her footsteps halted, which in turn caused him to stop beside her.

She asked, "This is where you lived with Diego?"

"That's right. This is where my mother left me."

Suddenly the house, the land, everything around her took on even more importance. When Laramie had told her they were coming to his place, she'd simply assumed it was a piece of property he'd purchased. Instead, it was a legacy, a symbol of his childhood. The notion touched her deeply.

"Diego willed this homestead to you?"

"He had no one else. He'd never been married. And when he died, his two brothers had already passed on. He truly considered me his son."

Curving his hand around her elbow, he urged her toward the front of the house. "Come on. I'll show you the inside," he said.

After guiding her to the door, she stood to one side while he opened the lock.

"I don't go in the house very often," he admitted. "So you'll have to ignore the dust."

"When you're used to living in a house with a leaky roof and broken plumbing, a little dust is nothing," she assured him.

With a hand at her back, he ushered her over the narrow threshold and into the very dark interior.

"Just wait here until I light a lamp. I don't keep the electricity turned on. With no one staying here it's not needed. And I don't have to worry about the wiring shorting out and starting a fire."

She heard the strike of a match and then a dim glow of light filled the room. Blinking her eyes to adjust to the semi-darkness, she glanced over to see Laramie standing next to a small table where he'd lit a kerosene lamp with a glass globe. She could see a dark green couch with sagging cushions behind him. Across from it sat a tall wooden rocker with a short footstool in front of it. It was the only furniture in the room.

Leyla stepped forward as she gazed curiously around her. "Is this the way things looked when you lived here?"

"No. There was a bit more furniture then. And things like newspapers and boots and ropes were always lying around. And a few beer cans, too. Diego liked his beer. But he never had one too many. He was a good man."

"You didn't have to tell me that. It's plain to me."

Curiosity arched one of his dark brows. "How did you come to that conclusion?"

"He raised you," she answered simply.

Her compliment put a modest grin on his face. "Diego would thank you for that. And so do I."

Something in his gaze reminded her that they were alone and that he was thinking about kissing her. Just as much as she was thinking about kissing him.

Doing her best to shake her mind from that temptation, she stepped away from him and forced her attention back to the bare, dusty room. "Was Diego originally from this area?" she asked.

"No. Fort Stockton. When he was about twenty-three or so he moved down here to Lincoln County to hunt for a job. He ended up going to work at the training barns at Ruidoso Downs. He'd done a bit of everything there. Mucking stalls, saddle valet, general gofer or whatever was needed. He stayed there for many years before he finally managed to gather enough money to buy this place. By then he was getting close to the age when most men retire. But to Diego he was just beginning. He never thought of himself as old. I guess that's why he was willing to take on the task of raising a baby."

Leyla couldn't stop her thoughts from straying to her own father. The man had never put much effort into being a father, an employee or even a husband. If he had, Leyla's life would have probably taken a different path. Not that she could blame George Chee for the mistakes she made with Heath. No, those had been her own. But a child, no matter what age, often needed a father's support. And that was something she'd never received from George Chee.

Across from her, she saw Laramie pick up the lamp then motion for her to follow him. "Come along and I'll show you the kitchen."

They stepped into a tiny hallway with three separate doors leading off from it. Laramie gestured to their right. "That's the bathroom and bedroom there. There's only one of each. Diego and I shared both."

She followed him through the open doorway to their left and into the kitchen, where plain, beige-colored cabinets filled one wall. Centered in the worn countertop was a single sink with a rusty water stain directly below the faucet. Along the adjoining wall was a small gas cook stove and an old refrigerator with the door propped open.

On the opposite side of the room there was a farm table with two worn chairs. Even with the furniture and appliances, the room looked bare and forgotten. To Leyla the notion was a sad one. The house had once been filled with life. A man and his son had dwelled here together. Now there was no one.

"Being in this house must bring up all sorts of memories of your father," she murmured as she gazed around the room where Laramie had taken his meals as a child. "Does it bother you to come inside?"

His life had changed dramatically from those days, she thought. Maybe seeing all this made him count his blessings.

After carefully placing the lamp on the table, he answered. "For a long time I couldn't walk into the house without it hurting. Right here." He bumped his fist against the middle of his chest. "But now I mostly remember and wonder."

The raw huskiness of his voice drew on her and as she moved closer, the warmth and scent of him added to the powerful pull of his presence. And suddenly she very much wanted to slip her arms around his lean waist and press her cheek against that spot on his chest that had once ached.

"Wonder?" she asked softly. "About what?"

Glancing at her, he shrugged. "Lots of things. Like where I really came from. And how Diego actually took guardianship over me."

Frowning, she studied his face. "I don't understand. I thought you knew how you came to live with Diego."

His expression wry, he shook his head. "I only know what I was told by Diego."

"And you doubt his word?"

With a rueful groan, he walked over to a door that led to the backyard. He opened it wide and Leyla wondered if he needed to see the cheery sunlight and hear the happy twittering of birds to push away the dark thoughts in his head.

"Like I said before, Diego was a good man. I never once knew of him lying to me about anything—until a few years ago when I got the idea to search for the whereabouts of my parents. It was then I learned that some of his story about my birth didn't ring true."

Surprised, she said, "If I remember right, you told me you didn't know your parents or where they might be."

Walking back to where she stood by the table, he said, "I still don't. I asked several old-timers in the area about Peggy Choney and if they remembered her. Some did. And they remember her being pregnant. But they had no idea where she'd gone to. And all the public records I could find have no trace of her."

Frowning thoughtfully, she asked, "Do you know how Peggy came to be acquainted with Diego?"

He nodded. "She worked as a waitress over in a little café in Alto. It was a place Diego frequented during his many trips to Ruidoso. Apparently they became friends and he helped her rent a little house that was situated about a mile from this one. That's how they ended up being neighbors."

"Is the house still standing? Does anyone live there now?"

He shook his head. "No. It's been torn down. When we drive back out, I'll show you where it used to be. It sat just off the road."

"Oh, so no clues there," she mused aloud. "But if Peggy and Diego were that close of friends, then he surely must have known the identity of your father."

"He always told me my father was a man named Calvin Jones. And that Peggy had met him while she'd been in Texas visiting family. The way he'd told it, she'd gotten pregnant by the man after a one-night stand." Releasing a heavy sigh, he lifted his hat and ran a hand through his dark hair. "But the story doesn't stand up."

"How do you know? Do you have proof that it happened differently?"

"Partly."

"What does that mean?

He shook his head with misgivings and Leyla wondered why he'd decided to tell her all of this now. It was clear that the whole matter tore deeply at him. Is that what he wanted her to see? That she wasn't the only one who'd been hurt by family?

"While Diego was still alive I didn't question his story.

I didn't want to insult the man who'd been such a good father to me by calling him a liar. And back then I had no means to search for Peggy or Calvin through computer or any other way. Later, after Diego passed away, I was too focused on making a home for myself at the Chaparral to worry about my long-lost parents. But a few years ago, Quint urged me to make an effort to search for information."

"And you found something." She stated the obvious.

"Hmm. I guess you could say it was what I didn't find that shed a different light on Diego's facts of the story."

"What does that mean?"

"Calvin was supposed to have been in the Army, stationed at Fort Bliss. And shortly after I was born Peggy decided to let Calvin know he had a son. That's when she'd learned he'd been killed in a training accident on the fort. The incident involved a helicopter, and Calvin had been badly burned. But I discovered all of that turned out to be false. The Army had no records of Calvin Jones being stationed at Fort Bliss at that time, much less one who had been killed in a helicopter crash."

Stunned by this revelation, Leyla's fingertips crept to her lips. "Oh, my. Calvin Jones didn't exist. At least, not Calvin the soldier in Texas. Did you discover any sort of clues to tell you who your father really was?"

Laramie said bleakly, "It's pretty obvious that without Peggy Choney, I'll never know."

Another idea suddenly struck her and she turned a hopeful look on him. "What about your birth certificate, Laramie? Maybe some of the information on it might give you clues. Ones that you never thought of before."

His lips spread to a thin line. "As far as I know the document is legitimate. But hell, enough money in the right place can buy anything. And there's no reason I can figure why a fake would be needed. Peggy had the right to list any name as my father."

"That's true," Leyla told him, then added, "I didn't have to produce Heath when the hospital made out Dillon's birth certificate. But something else about all of this puzzles me even more, Laramie. Why did Peggy go off and leave you with Diego?"

Shrugging, he turned slightly away from her but not before Leyla saw the flat, empty look on his face. "I'm not sure I'll ever know the real truth of that, either. Diego says she was so distraught when she found out about Calvin's death that she went out of her head. She asked him to watch her baby while she went off to try to gather herself together. She told him she'd come back as soon as she could, but she never returned."

There was no anger or bitterness in his voice. Just a fatal resignation that tore at her. "Oh, Laramie," she said in a half-whisper. "There was no Calvin. So what could have been going on with her?"

"There's no way of knowing now," he said lowly. "But it's clear she left me with Diego for some reason instead of putting me up for adoption."

Moving closer, Leyla curled her hand around his forearm. "Laramie, that makes me think—well, maybe Diego was your real father and the two of them wanted to keep the fact hidden for some reason?"

"I suppose that could be possible. But I'd say it's doubtful. Peggy was very young. Only twenty-one or so whenever she gave birth to me. At that time Diego was in his sixties. He liked to consider himself young and fit—but not in that way. He wouldn't have gotten involved with a woman that young. It just wasn't his nature at all. In fact, the people around who still remember Peggy say that Diego treated her more like a daughter than anything."

"Hmm. Well, that would go along with the fact that he helped her rent a house rather than have her move in with him. But what reason does a woman have for leaving her child? Fear? Insecurity? I'm a mother and I can't think of any reason I'd ever leave Dillon."

The anguish on his face tore at Leyla and as she ached for him, she realized that Laramie had become much more to her than a sexy, desirable man who was kind to her and her son. She wanted him to be happy, to feel loved and wanted and worthwhile. She wanted that for him as much as she wanted it for herself and Dillon.

Oh, God, had she already fallen in love with him and was just now realizing it? The answer to that left her shaking inside.

Moving closer, she rested her palms against his chest. "Laramie, I don't understand. Did you bring me here just to tell me all of this? If you did, you wasted your time. This stuff about your parents—yes, I wish that you knew the truth. Just so it would ease your mind. But the man you are now is what matters the most to me."

The grateful look in his eyes filled her with relief. She didn't want this man to suffer for any reason. Certainly not because of his past.

"I'm glad you feel that way. But I actually brought you here for a different reason. I mean—yes, you needed to know about Peggy and the story Diego told me. Otherwise, you wouldn't understand why I keep this place. Why it will always be a part of me. But it's not my home."

"Laramie, I—"

Her words halted as his hands quickly lifted to frame the sides of her face.

"Leyla, just wait. Let me finish before you say anything. You need to understand that for years this was my home. We had food in the cupboards, clothes on our backs and a bit of livestock but not much more. After Diego died, I was lost—just a big kid with no one to guide me. You see, this place was empty without him."

With his hands on her face and the front of his body pressed against hers, she could hardly focus on his words. She wanted to tell him that they'd talked enough. That all she wanted was his mouth on hers, his arms drawing her closer and his embrace making her forget the sorrows they'd both been through.

Battling the risky thoughts in her head, she stated the obvious, "You went to the Chaparral. But why there?"

"While Diego was drawing his last breaths, he made me promise that I would go to the Chaparral and ask Lewis for a job. He'd said that Lewis was an old friend of his and that he would do right by me. I didn't question him about the matter. And I sure wasn't about to break the promise I'd made to Diego. A few days after Diego's funeral, I went."

"Had you met any of the Cantrells before?"

He paused and shook his head. "Quint and I went to the same high school and I'd vaguely remembered his sister, Alexa, graduating a few years before. But I didn't know either of them personally. Hell, when I went to the big ranch I was just a scared kid with two years of high school to finish. I'll never understand why, but Lewis took me under his wing and helped me become a part of the ranch and a part of his family."

"And after that the Chaparral became your home. I understand that," she said softly.

His gaze caught hers and held it. "I guess what I'm trying to say is—well, this place legally belongs to me. I could pour money into it and build it up into a nice little ranch, but it wouldn't be home to me. Can you understand how I feel?"

Her throat tight with emotions, she turned her back to

him. Tears rarely ever filled Leyla's eyes. She'd decided crying couldn't fix things. But now she found herself fighting back a wall of tears.

"I understand that you'll never leave the Chaparral," she said huskily. "Not for any reason."

She heard his groan of frustration, then felt his hands settle on her shoulders and it was all Leyla could do to keep from turning and flinging her arms around him. A part of her was aching to tell him she didn't care where she lived or what she did so long as he was at her side. But she bit down on the words and refused to let them roll from her tongue. Because she knew that once she ever said them, the dreams she'd held on to for so long would all be shattered.

"Leyla, I realize you want a home of your own and—"

Squeezing her eyes shut, she said, "Laramie, that's not your concern. Dillon and I will soon be gone and eventually we'll get that place of our own."

His hands tightened on her shoulders. "That's just it, Leyla. I don't want you to leave." Slowly, he turned her so that she was facing him and her heart jerked as she spotted the smoldering light in his eyes. "Surely you can tell that I care about you—that you can feel how much I want you."

Care. It wasn't the same as love, but he was sincere. Somehow she knew that and his honesty was more than she'd ever had from any man. It was enough to give her the courage to slip her arms around his waist and tilt her head back so that she could look him squarely in the eyes.

"After Heath I swore I'd never let another man touch me. But I—" The soft sigh that passed her lips was clearly a sound of surrender. "I want you, too, Laramie."

His eyes searched hers as his hands slipped from her shoulders and slid down her bare arms. Behind the trail of his fingertips, goose bumps covered her skin.

"The other night you talked about being afraid when I kissed you. I—"

She interrupted, "I was scared then. Because you made me feel so much. And I knew if I let myself I— We'd get carried away."

One hand lifted and as he stroked her hair gently away from her face, a wave of desire swept through her. It burned her cheeks and sent her heart on a drunken gallop.

"Oh, Leyla," he murmured, "would that be so bad?"

"I've been telling myself I'd be stupid to let you make love to me. But right now everything about being here with you like this feels good—special."

Slowly his head descended toward hers. "I honestly didn't bring you here to seduce you."

"I never thought that you had." She tightened her hold on his waist and as their bodies moved closer together, she could feel the bulge of his desire pressing against her. The sensation made her forget all the reasons she shouldn't make love to this man. Instead, it reminded her that no matter what misery she'd endured these past four years, she was still a woman with a woman's needs. And right now, they were too strong, too compelling to ignore. "You don't have to seduce me, Laramie. I'm already here in your arms."

Beneath the veil of her lashes, she watched his lips mouth her name and then he closed the last bit of distance between their faces. When his lips finally made contact with hers, an explosion of sensations rocked her senses and all she could do was cling to him and let his kiss draw her into a swirling vortex.

Instantly, the intimate contact turned to a hot, out-of-control mating of their mouths. Tongues tangled and lips searched for relief from the grip of desire that had over-taken both of them. Leyla had never been kissed so recklessly or completely. The intensity robbed her ability to think or even breathe. If she hadn't been gripping his back, she would have fallen.

Once his lips finally eased away from hers, her lungs were heaving for air and her face burned from the heat that was consuming her body.

"Leyla," he whispered, "do you know what that kiss was telling me?"

He was giving her a chance to change her mind, she thought. A chance to walk out of the house and end the desire that had been simmering inside her almost from the first day she'd met him. Stopping things now might be the sensible thing to do. But then she would never know what it meant to be in Laramie's arms, to experience the pleasure of making love to him. And to miss that chance would be a loss that would haunt her the rest of her life.

"It was saying I want you to make love to me," she said in a breathless rush.

His eyes were suddenly glowing as though she'd just handed him a gift.

"Leyla," he murmured. "Sweet Leyla."

His hands held her face as he bent to kiss her again. But this time he didn't allow the kiss to go on and on like the first one. Instead, he wasted no time in scooping her up in his arms and carrying her out of the room.

Chapter Ten

Laramie carried her out of the kitchen, down the tiny hallway and through a door to their left. When he set her feet back on the floor, Leyla could see they were standing next to a double bed. The sagging mattress was covered by a thin, faded blue spread. Two pillows in plain white cases were propped against the iron rail headboard.

"This isn't the place I would've chosen for this," he said. "But it'll have to do."

He moved around the room to a small window and partially opened the wooden shutters. Fresh air and sunlight came streaming in, along with a symphony of birdsongs. When he returned to Leyla, he pulled her into the loose circle of his arms, and as his hands gently roamed the contours of her back, the soft, kneading pressure of his fingers sent licks of fire through Leyla.

Glancing at the bed, she tried to reassure him. "I'm not used to special things."

"We could shake out the spread, but I figure that would only stir up the dust worse."

A faint smile touched her lips. As far as she was concerned, being in a luxurious bedroom on a romantic island couldn't make these moments with him any more special. And with a sense of amazement, she wondered how she'd been able to resist this man until now. "I can stand a little dust."

With a grunt of pleasure, he said, "I knew all along you were my kind of woman."

Mesmerized, she watched the grin slowly fall from his face. Her heart pounded with anticipation as his head bent and he pressed kisses across her cheeks and nose, then on her closed eyelids.

The sweet sensations drew sighs of pleasure from her until his lips formed a hot seal over hers. After that her sighs turned to deep groans and before she realized it, his fingers were inching down the zipper at the back of her dress.

When the garment fell from her shoulders and pooled around her ankles, she felt a sense of freedom, and not just from a barrier of clothing. She felt free to let herself feel again, to be a whole woman again.

"You're perfect, Leyla. Perfect and lovely," he whispered as he stood gazing down at the image she made in a set of white, lacy underwear. "Ever since I met you that first night, I've pictured you like this. You're more beautiful than I imagined."

His bold gaze didn't make her feel self-conscious, but something about hearing him say the compliment put a blush on her face. "I'm very average," she denied.

Grinning, he slipped his thumbs beneath her bra straps and guided them down her shoulders. "I've never had any problem with my eyesight, Leyla."

As he spoke the last words, the lacy cups fell from her breasts and she gasped as his hands closed around the sensitive mounds of flesh. Her head rolled to one side and as his thumb and forefingers teased her nipples, his lips sought the curve of her exposed neck.

As he kissed his way down to the curve of her shoulder, the ache of wanting him pierced her loins and spread to the intimate spot between her legs. The sweet agony had her groaning with need and arching her body into his.

As her hands sought the buttons on the front of his shirt, she whispered frantically, "I need to touch you, Laramie. Please let me."

His hands shaking now, he pushed hers out of the way and jerked the tails of his denim shirt out of the waistband of his jeans. As soon as they were free, he ripped the pearl snaps apart, then shrugged out of the garment and flung it aside.

He wore no undershirt and for one split second Leyla could only stare at the wide, muscled chest that narrowed down to a lean waist. His skin was brown, his flat nipples a shade darker. There was no patch of hair growing between them, but a faint line of fine black hair marked the indention between his abs, then disappeared below the waist of his jeans.

Awed by the sight of him, her hands settled against his ribcage, then slid slowly up and over his hot skin until they reached the bulge of pectoral muscles. There her fingers tweaked his nipples until they became two hard buttons.

"Oh, Leyla, honey, I can't take this."

His voice was thick with desire and the sound empowered Leyla even more. Just to know that she could arouse this man, that he could want her this much, filled her with a sense of confidence and gave her the courage to allow her actions to convey her wants.

She brought her lips against one of the nipples. "What about this?" she whispered.

Not waiting for his answer, she softly bit the tiny nub, then followed that with a moist kiss that left her tongue lathing his flesh.

Above her head, she heard a deep groan in his throat and then his fingers were in her hair, tearing at the pins holding the heavy coil in place. Once it was loose, he grabbed up fistful of strands and used them to draw her face back up to his.

With his lips against hers, he spoke roughly, "I can't hold on, Leyla. Not like that."

"I don't want you to hold on," she said in a rush.

He closed the space between their lips, but as soon as the kiss grew out of control, he broke the intimate contact and reached for her underwear. Once the scrap of material was out of the way, he placed her on the mattress and slipped off her sandals.

Her heart pounding with anticipation, Leyla watched him as he sat on the side of the bed to pull off his boots. After the second thump on the floor, he stood and quickly removed the remainder of his clothing.

As he lowered himself next to her on the mattress, Leyla realized she should feel some sort of embarrassment at seeing Laramie in an undressed state and especially at her decision to go to bed with him. But as he pulled her into the tight circle of his arms and the front of his body pressed against hers, she felt nothing but mindless pleasure.

Once his mouth fastened over hers and his hands began to urgently search the contours of her body, Leyla's thoughts closed off to everything but him and the need to be closer.

When she slipped her leg over his hips and drew the bottom half of her body next to his, the silent invitation caused his head to ease back far enough to look at her. "Leyla, this is awkward, but do I need to wear protection? I wasn't planning for this."

Placing her palm alongside his face, her gaze delved deeply into his. "Ever since I gave birth to Dillon, I've taken oral contraceptives. Not because I needed them but because I was afraid. Afraid that I'd not learned my lesson. That I'd meet someone and have a weak moment. Or I'd meet someone who pretended to care but really didn't."

His roving hand stilled upon her hip. "You didn't trust yourself. Or men," he said knowingly. "What about now? Me?"

Her throat tightened with raw need. Not just to couple her body to his, but from the need to love him with all her heart. "I don't have any choice, Laramie. I want you too much."

Something gentle and caring flickered in his eyes and then his lips were against her cheek, softly mouthing her name. Her heart melting, Leyla wrapped her arms around his neck and urged him to make the connection between them complete. He didn't deny her.

Rolling her onto her back, he braced himself over her and she parted her legs, inviting him to end the throbbing agony. With his head thrown back, his gaze holding on to hers, he pushed himself into the moist folds of her womanhood. The pleasurable shock rippled through her like gentle waves on a smooth pond.

"Leyla. My darling."

His low voice vibrated with the intensity of his desire and the sound brought a sting of tears to her eyes. Quickly, she closed them and buried her face against his shoulder.

"Love me, Laramie. Love me."

His hips thrust against hers. Slowly at first, then faster and faster. Leyla matched the needy rhythm and the friction acted like wind on a forest fire. There was no stopping the flames from tearing through their bodies. The only way to end it now was to let the fire burn itself out.

Leyla couldn't hold back or hide her need for him. She clung to him while meeting his open-mouthed kisses with a recklessness that stunned her. And then as she fought to get closer, even as she found herself climbing higher and higher, she realized she was craving much more than this man's body. She loved him. Loved him with every particle in her body.

The fact hit her at the same moment her body was splintering into a shower of lights, and the combination of her body and heart merging into one, loving and giving at the same time, caused her to sob his name over and over.

He responded by clasping her head to his chest and burying his face in the top of her hair. She felt herself floating off to a soft place where there was nothing but him and her together. Always together.

Moments later, his body drenched in sweat and his lungs still working hard to return to normal, Laramie shifted his weight off Leyla but kept a firm hold on her waist. Even now with his senses slowly returning, she was the most solid thing in the room. And he didn't want to let her go. Ever.

He wasn't sure what had just happened between them. Even though he'd thought about making love to Leyla a million and one times, he'd certainly not planned or expected it to happen today. Hell, he figured it would take a miracle for her to ever fall in bed with him. But from the moment they'd left the ranch to drive over here, he'd sensed something different in the way she'd looked at him, touched him. And then when they'd kissed it was like the world around them had exploded. She'd not held back then and she sure hadn't held back just now. Merely thinking about the way she'd responded, giving every part of herself to him, was enough to curl his toes and stir his exhausted body.

Admit it, Laramie, it was more than her body that rocked you. When you held her, when you poured your seed into her, your heart opened and she slipped inside it. You love her. If you hadn't known it before, you know it now.

Laramie didn't try to suppress the little voice going off in his head. There wasn't any use in trying to deny what it was saying. The question now was what he intended to do about it.

"I'm so sorry, Leyla."

His words came out on a strangled sort of whisper, but she heard them and turned her head to look at him. Her dark eyes were glazed with moisture, her lips swollen from the kisses he'd placed upon them. Drops of perspiration dotted her forehead and dampened her hairline. She was so lovely, he thought. So soft and gentle. She was everything he'd ever wanted in a woman and it amazed him that she was here beside him like this.

"You're sorry because this happened?"

He turned onto his side so that he was facing her. "That's not what I meant at all. I'm sorry that it happened here in this dusty old house instead of someplace special. You deserve that, Leyla."

A faint smile tilted her lips and Laramie couldn't stop himself from bending and placing a soft kiss on one corner. A musky, sensual scent drifted from her hair and mingled with the womanly smell of her body. Laramie inhaled and reveled in its pleasure.

"You make it special for me, Laramie. Don't you know that by now?"

Laramie often received praise for his work, his horses and the dedication he showed to his friends. But Leyla's remark was something totally different, something he'd never heard from anyone before, especially a woman. The fact that it was coming from Leyla made it even more incredible.

His chest swelling with tender emotion, he nuzzled her cheek with his lips. "I can't begin to tell you how you make me feel, Leyla. These past few hours—they'll be forever burned in my memory. I'll never forget them. Ever."

She didn't say anything and he eased his head back so that he could look at her face. To his dismay tears filled her eyes and were very close to spilling over onto her cheek. The sight of them cut him deeply. He never wanted Leyla to cry or hurt over anything. She'd already suffered too much in her young life.

"Leyla! What's wrong? I've messed everything up, haven't I? I've hurt you—"

The emphatic shake of her head halted the remainder of his words and he stared, bewildered by this sudden change in her.

"You've not hurt me. I was just thinking about—things. About this. You and me. And Dillon."

Suddenly she closed her eyes, then quickly rolled away from him and sat up on the edge of the bed. "We'd better be going, don't you think?" she said, her voice low and stiff. "Sassy will be expecting us back very soon."

He didn't want to go. He wanted to pull her back into his arms and make love to her all over again. He wanted to hear her whimpers of desire, feel her body telling him how much she needed him. The way she was at this moment made it feel as though there was a deep, rocky canyon between them.

Pushing himself up from the mattress, he raked both

hands through his tousled hair and tried to compose his rattled senses. In a matter of minutes he'd gone from euphoria to confusion.

"If that's what you want," he said.

"What I want has nothing to do with it," she reasoned. "I have a son—responsibilities."

A spurt of anger suddenly rifled through him. "I have plenty of responsibilities, too. And I figure when I turn my phone back on, I'll be blasted with calls and messages from people needing me. But that doesn't mean you and I don't deserve a few minutes together. We are human."

Blinking at the tears in her eyes, she bent over to retrieve her sundress from the floor. "We just proved we're human, Laramie, and I wish we had a few more minutes to share like this, but we don't."

Standing, she stepped into the garment and Laramie reached to zip the back of it together. Once the task was finished, he rested his hands on her shoulders.

"Leyla, I'm going to ask you the same question you asked me a few moments ago. Are you sorry this happened?"

Groaning with anguish, she turned and buried her face against his chest. Laramie closed his eyes and held her tightly.

"No! I'm not sorry, Laramie." Tilting her neck back, she looked up at him. "I think I'm scared. Scared of what you're starting to mean to me."

He shook his head. "There's no need for you to be afraid. I've told you before, Leyla—I'll never hurt you."

Biting down on her lip, she glanced away from him. "That's not exactly what scares me. You're not like Heath—I can see that. But I can see that your life is on the Chaparral. And that's so far away from nursing school and all the things I'd planned for myself, my son and aunt."

Laramie wanted to set her down, to explain that what they'd shared on the bed behind them had been more than just incredible sex to him. He needed to tell her that he'd fallen in love with her, that his future wouldn't be complete unless she and Dillon were in it. But something told him that now was not the time or place. When he did reveal his feelings to her, he wanted them to be on the Chaparral. Because the ranch was his home. It was who he was. And if she couldn't accept it as her permanent home, too, then there was little hope for their relationship to flourish.

"Okay. We'll talk about that later. We'll get you back to Dillon now." Bending, he placed a kiss on her forehead. "If you want to freshen up before we leave, there's water in the bathroom. It works on gravity flow."

"Thank you," she whispered, then grabbed her sandals and quickly left the room.

On the drive home, Leyla sat quietly gazing out at the landscape, seemingly lost in her thoughts. It was clear their moments of closeness were over. At least for the time being. Before they'd left the little stucco house, Laramie had turned his phone back on and now, as he negotiated the truck over the rough dirt road, it began to ring incessantly.

At first he ignored it. Like Leyla, he wasn't really in the mood to talk, but after a moment she looked at him and said, "Something must be wrong. Maybe you should answer it."

Deciding she was probably right, he reached for the phone and immediately spotted Quint's number illuminated on the ID. "I'm here," he answered. "What is it?"

"Where the hell is 'here'?" Quint demanded. "I've been trying to reach you for the past hour!"

Laramie didn't let the other man's ire get to him. He'd learned long ago that Quint was wired to a different gear than Laramie moved in. Whereas Quint grew hot and bothered in the flash of an eye, Laramie normally remained cool and steady.

"I had something personal to do. I turned off my phone for a while."

A stretch of silence passed and Laramie figured his explanation had taken the other man aback. It wasn't often that he took time away from the ranch for "personal" reasons. And no one was more aware of that than Quint.

"Oh. Well, I'm here at the Chaparral waiting on you. I've got to drive up to the Pine Ridge ranch and try to smooth his hackles. I need you to go with me. You can talk to the bastard more sensibly than I can."

"Yeah, you probably should take me. Otherwise you might wind up in jail on assault charges."

Quint chuckled, then after a pause said, "Sorry for barking at you. I've had a lot on my plate here lately."

"Forget it. I know your plate is overloaded right now. Bark all you want. I'll be there in twenty minutes."

"You can find me at the vet barn."

After punching the end button on the phone, Laramie tossed the instrument into an open storage cavity on the console. As he pushed down the accelerator and sent the truck speeding on down the dirt road, Leyla asked guardedly, "Is someone in trouble? You mentioned something about jail."

He shot her a patient grin. "That was a joke. The trouble isn't that bad. At least I don't think it is."

"I hope not," she said with concern.

He let out a heavy sigh. Before Leyla came into his life, he never resented the interference of his work. But she was changing him, making him realize he needed more than keeping a crew of ranch hands busy and a few thousand cattle healthy.

"One of these days we're going to find out who's responsible for all this sabotage," he said flatly. "And then there's going to be some hell to pay."

From the corner of his eye he saw her frown. Maybe he shouldn't have said anything about the problem, he thought. But if he ever expected her to understand his life, she needed to know everything it entailed. And right now some of it wasn't pretty.

"Do you ever worry that these incidents—or whatever you call them—might turn into something more dangerous?"

"To tell you the truth, Leyla, I almost expect it. Anybody who can poison a baby calf is a very disturbed person. So far he's gotten away with this stuff. That's going to make him bolder. But I look at it this way—in the end evil always destroys itself."

"That's true," she agreed. "But what happens in the meantime?"

The uncertain look on her face had him reaching over and squeezing her hand. "I don't want you to worry, Leyla. Not about anything. Especially about me or you. Or us."

She cast him a doubtful look. "Is there really an us, Laramie?"

"As far as I'm concerned there is."

She shook her head, then looked away from him. "I should have never went to bed with you," she said softly.

His boot unconsciously eased off the accelerator, making the truck slow to a crawl. "Why are you saying that?" he demanded. "You just told me you didn't regret it!"

"I know. And I don't. But I—" Her head twisted back around and she stared at him, her eyes full of anguish. "I didn't expect it would suddenly have you thinking of us as a couple!"

Frustration very nearly had him steering the truck to

the side of the road. He wanted like hell to pull her into his arms and tell her all the things he was feeling, all the things he was dreaming and hoping for the three of them. But he couldn't stop now. Quint was waiting.

"We're going to talk this out, Leyla," he said firmly. "But not now. After Quint and I get back from the Pine Ridge ranch."

Fifteen minutes later, they reached the Chaparral ranch house and Laramie dropped Leyla off at the backyard gate. When she entered the ranch house, the kitchen was empty, so she headed straight to her apartment. There she found Sassy watching television and Dillon sound asleep on the carpet.

Hearing the door open and close, Sassy looked over her shoulder as Leyla entered the room. "There you are," the maid said. "I was beginning to think you and Laramie had left the country."

Leyla could feel her cheeks warming with color. "We stayed out a little longer than we'd planned. I hope you haven't been in a big hurry to leave."

Batting a hand through the air, Sassy said, "Not at all. I love being with Dillon and there's nothing waiting on me at my place in town."

"Thanks," Leyla told her. "I promise I'll make it up to you."

Sassy chuckled. "Just getting to eat your pies and cakes are enough payment."

Leyla inclined her head toward Dillon. Has he been asleep for very long?"

"About five minutes. I started to move him to the couch, but he looked so comfortable I hated to disturb him."

"That's fine. He likes to sleep on the floor." She glanced

at the small toys scattered around her son. "Did he give you any problems?"

Sassy's smile was full of affection. "Not even one. We had fun playing ranch. Dillon wanted to be the boss. Like Laramie."

No matter where she went or what she did, she couldn't get away from the man. And to make matters worse, she didn't want to. Walking over to the couch, Leyla took a seat on an end cushion. "I'm not surprised."

"He talks about the man constantly. Have you noticed?"

Dillon talked about Laramie just as much as Leyla thought about him. And now, God help her, she'd fallen in love with him. She'd given him her body as though she were planning on being with him until the end of time.

What had she been thinking? He'd never said anything about love or marriage or forever. But he had implied he wanted her to stay on the ranch. And she instinctively knew he didn't want her to hang around just to have a torrid affair. He wasn't that sort of man. But even if he proposed marriage to her, how could she accept? The ranch was several miles of rough traveling just to get to a two-year college in Ruidoso. To become an RN, she'd have to travel far away to another city. There was also her aunt to consider. The woman was soon going to need a home and someone to care for her. How could she expect a man who'd been a bachelor for all these years to suddenly deal with all these family issues at once?

"I've noticed," she replied to the maid's remark.

Sassy aimed the remote at the television. Once it went quiet, she turned a sly grin on Leyla.

"I won't ask where you two went. But I will ask if you had a nice time."

Warmth filled Leyla's cheeks. Nice? The time she and Laramie had spent on that old iron post bed could hardly be called nice. Wild and incredible would be a better description.

"Yes. It was nice." Trying to appear as casual as possible, she tucked her legs beneath her and smoothed a hand over her skirt. Thankfully, before they'd left the little house she'd taken the time to redo her hair and makeup. She was confident that outwardly she looked the same. It was her insides that were different. She felt as if they'd been shaken to pieces, then shaped into something she didn't recognize. In a matter of a few short hours she'd learned so much about Laramie and about herself. Yet there was still so much she didn't know. And doubts about the future refused to leave her mind. "He wanted to show me a piece of property."

Sassy's frown was almost comical. "In the middle of the afternoon? With all that's been going on around this ranch, it must have been damned important. Quint stopped by the house a little earlier looking for him. He seemed pretty stressed about something."

Why had Laramie suddenly made an issue of taking her to see the place Diego had willed him?

He'd wanted you to learn about the uncertainty surrounding his birth and how he'd come to live in the little stucco. And most of all he wanted to make it clear that the Chaparral was his home now. A home he'd never leave.

Forcing herself to focus on Sassy's remark, she said, "He and Laramie are headed up to the Pine Ridge ranch. I think it's something to do about the cattle that strayed onto Pickens's land."

Sassy grimaced. "Hmm. Well, most neighboring ranchers are pretty understanding when that sort of thing happens, but from what I understand Pickens is a hothead."

Suddenly Laramie's remark about jail and assault charges made more sense. He and Quint must be expecting trouble out of their neighbor to the north. The notion sent a shiver down her spine. If anything happened to Laramie, it would tear her right in two and Dillon would be devastated. Her son wouldn't understand. Just like he hadn't understood when Laramie had been gone from the ranch for days during spring roundup.

Another thought suddenly struck her and she shot the maid a curious look. "Sassy, how do you know these things that go on around here? Are you dating one of the ranch hands?"

Sassy wrinkled her nose. "None on a steady basis. Like I told you, the one I want doesn't know I exist."

Leyla perceptively studied the other woman. "Are you talking about Laramie?"

Tilting back her head, Sassy let out a generous laugh. "There's no need for you to get jealous. Laramie is certainly a hunk of eye candy. But he's way too quiet and intense for my taste. I want a man who can make me laugh. Make me feel good and forget about my troubles."

Funny that the other woman should say that, Leyla thought. Laramie didn't just make her forget her troubles; he made her forget everything.

"Oh, by the way," Sassy continued. "Reena called while you were out. She said Jim is getting his cast off one day next week."

Even though the temperature in the apartment was pleasant, Leyla suddenly felt chilled and she unconsciously hugged her bare arms to her waist. Next week! When Quint had talked to her about taking this job, he'd told her to plan for at least two months of work. In the back of her mind, she'd been thinking that no matter what happened in the future, she still had a few weeks left to be with Laramie. Now it looked as though that time might be cut short.

The disappointment Leyla was feeling must have shown

on her face because Sassy quickly continued, "I wouldn't expect Reena to be coming back anytime soon, though. She said the doctor had ordered more X-rays to make sure everything was mended, and then Jim would need therapy."

Even so, it was clear that Jim was on the road to recovery. Reena would be returning in the not-too-distant future. When that happened, Leyla would no longer be needed. She'd come here knowing the circumstances of the job. Just because she'd fallen in love with Laramie didn't alter the situation.

Sighing, she rose to her feet and started gathering up the toys that Dillon had strewn around the room. "Well, I took this job with the understanding that it was temporary. The manager of the Blue Mesa promised to keep a slot open for me whenever I finished here." Clutching the toys to her aching chest, she glanced at Sassy and did her best to smile. "Everything will be fine. I'll just be leaving sooner than I expected."

Sassy appeared to be as disappointed over the news as Leyla felt. "You'll have to go back to that leaky house with broken plumbing. Have you started searching for a new rental yet?"

"No. I've been wondering if it would make more financial sense to have Aunt Oneida's house repaired. With a little luck I might get a loan for the improvements. Making those payments couldn't be any worse than doling out rent. And that way when my aunt leaves the nursing home, she'll get to return to her own home."

Shaking her head, Sassy rose to her feet. "Sounds nice for your aunt. But Leyla, how can you support the three of you on a waitress's salary?"

Leyla wasn't the type to stick her head in the sand and

pretend she had everything under control. But she wasn't going to let the problems crush her fighting spirit, either.

Smiling, she answered, "I'll manage somehow."

As Sassy helped her collect the last of the toys from the floor, she asked, "What about Dillon?"

Casting a cautious look at her friend, Leyla dropped an armful of plastic animals into a wooden toy box. "What about him?"

Joining her at the toy box, Sassy tossed in the last of the toys. "From what I can tell he's grown really attached to Laramie. And he loves it here."

Leyla bit back a sigh. "That fact goes through my mind all the time, Sassy."

The maid shot her a look that was both awkward and annoyed. "Well, don't you ever think that your son needs a daddy?"

Frowning, Leyla moved around the other woman and started toward the door that led out of the apartment. "I'm going to the kitchen. I need something to drink," she muttered.

Sassy followed quickly on her heels and as they entered the quiet kitchen, the maid said, "Look, Leyla, I'm not trying to stick my nose in your personal affairs, but I just don't get you. Or maybe I'm wrong in thinking you're falling for Laramie."

Leyla whirled around to stare at Sassy. Since she'd come to the Chaparral, she'd grown close to this bubbly, red-haired woman. But she'd certainly never talked about her personal feelings about Laramie to her. How had the woman guessed? Was she wearing the fact on her face? Oh, Lord, maybe Sassy could tell she'd spent part of the afternoon making passionate love to the ranch foreman.

"Falling for Laramie? I've only been here three weeks!" She walked toward the coffeemaker.

"If you're looking at the right man, you'll know it in three hours or three days. It sure as heck shouldn't take three weeks!"

Leyla fitted the coffeemaker with a filter and grounds. "I'm not you, Sassy. Besides, I'm not looking to have a long-term relationship with Laramie. He's—"

"Crazy about you!"

Not daring to look at Sassy, Leyla added water to the machine and flipped on the switch. He'd certainly made love to her like he'd meant it. But that had been physical, she mentally argued.

"You couldn't know that. You've never even seen the two of us in the same room together," Leyla shot back at her, then sighed. "Sorry, Sassy. I didn't mean to sound short."

"And I don't mean to pry. I just want you and little Dillon to be happy, that's all. And if Laramie is offering you a place in his life, then what could be better?"

Keeping her back to her friend, she swallowed hard. "He's not offering me a place in his life, Sassy. So quit dreaming. I did a long time ago."

But Leyla couldn't quit hoping. She had to believe that this time in her life she would make the right choices for her and Dillon. Even if those choices broke her heart.

Chapter Eleven

When Laramie finally finished dealing with Quint and their irate neighbor, he still had to make sure the ranch hands had all the fences intact and every stray animal back where it should be. By the time he returned to the ranch house, the hour was growing late.

Inside the kitchen the smells of cooked food still lingered, but he didn't stop to satisfy his empty stomach. Leyla was on his mind and he wouldn't get a wink of sleep if he didn't see her tonight.

To his relief, he could see a shaft of light beneath her door and she answered his knock fairly quickly. The sight of her standing on the other side of the threshold, her petite curves wrapped in a plain cotton robe, was a feast to his eyes.

"May I come in?" he asked.

"Of course." She pushed the door wider and he stepped

inside the quiet little living room. "Did you find your supper?"

"I didn't bother to look," he admitted, then glanced past her shoulder at the quiet room. "Is Dillon already in bed?"

She nodded. "I never allow him to stay up this late. Why do you ask? Did you want to see him?"

Shaking his head, Laramie reached and pulled her into the circle of his arms. Once the front of her body was crushed up against his, he answered her question. "No. I wanted to see you. That's all I've been thinking about."

"It was getting so late I didn't think I'd see you tonight," she admitted. "Did everything go okay with Pickens?"

"I don't want to talk about that now." His hands roamed her back, his fingers playing with her loose black hair. It was coarse and straight and shiny enough to have been spun with sunshine. He lifted a stand to his nose and breathed in the delicate scent. "In fact, I don't want to talk at all."

"Laramie, you said—"

"I plan on saying a lot of things—just give me time," he murmured, his mouth descending toward hers.

For a split second he thought she might want to argue that point, but then her eyelids drifted downward and her lips parted in anticipation.

Groaning with utter pleasure, Laramie closed the fraction of distance between their lips. The contact was an explosion, nearly rocking him back on his heels, and when her fingers thrust into his hair, he knew she was feeling the same incredible hunger.

Just touching her like this aroused him, filled him with a desperate ache to be inside her. He'd never had anything affect him so swiftly or deeply and the realization stunned him, frightened him with its intensity.

Tearing his mouth from hers, he whispered against her

ear. "Do you have another bedroom? Besides the one Dillon is in?"

Nodding, she took him by the hand and led him to the far end of the room where a door opened into a bedroom with a view to the back patio. Through the parted drapes he could see a crescent moon hanging over a jagged edge of mountain and silver light flickered through the boughs of a ponderosa pine.

Leyla released her hold on his hand and walked over to the nightstand to switch on a small lamp. A golden hue suddenly spread over a double bed covered by a patchwork quilt and two pillows encased in lacy shams. Laramie could hardly wait to get Leyla spread out on the smooth covers, to have her warm softness pressed against him.

In two strides he was at her side, untying the belt on her robe, only to have her halt his busy fingers.

"Wait," she whispered. "I'll shut the door. Just in case Dillon should wake."

As he watched her deal with the door, he asked, "Does Dillon often wake at night?"

"Never. I guess he plays so hard it makes him sleep soundly."

She returned to his side and he leaned over and switched off the lamp. "I want to see you washed with moonlight," he said softly.

With the light off, he turned back to her and quickly slipped the robe from her body. Beneath the garment she was totally nude, and the sight of her small, sensual curves pulled a groan of pleasure from his throat.

"Quint accused me of drinking this evening. And I couldn't blame him. It was hell following his conversation and I asked him to repeat himself a half dozen times." His hands skimmed over her smooth, heated skin, along the slopes and valleys that made up her body. "I couldn't explain to him that I was drunk on you. That all I could think about was getting you back in my arms. It's crazy how much I want you, Leyla."

Laying her on the bed, he quickly shed his clothing then joined her on the cool quilt. She settled into his arms with a sigh and he quickly brought his lips down on hers. He kissed her until deep moans filled her throat and the agony gripping his body became too much to bear.

When he rolled her onto her back and straddled her, she looked up at him, her eyes shining with a tender light that melted his very bones. She had to love him. She just had to. Otherwise, he would be empty.

The desperate thought raced through his mind as he quickly connected his body to hers. But once he'd sunk himself deep within her, his mind lost all thought except pushing the two of them to that special place. A place he'd never visited until this afternoon when she'd led him into a secret wonderland.

Much later, after the heat of their passion had run its course, Laramie tucked her into the protective curve of his body and murmured in a drained voice, "Now I can talk. We can talk."

His hand was resting against her stomach and she threaded her fingers through his. "I thought that's what we'd been doing," she said.

Smiling with pleasure, he nuzzled his face against the side of her silky hair. "That was body talk. I need to speak words. I need to say things I should have said back at the house before we…well, before we—"

His search for the right words halted as she twisted her body around so that their faces were only inches apart and her pert little breasts were crushed against his chest.

"Had sex," she finished for him.

Disappointment tugged the corners of his lips downward. "That wasn't having sex. Not to me. It was making love."

A guarded look washed over her face. "That's a big difference, Laramie."

Sighing, he pulled his fingers from hers and used them to comb her tousled hair back from her brow. "I want you to understand that I'm not here with you like this just because I want to have sex with you. I love you, Leyla."

Even in the semi-darkness he could see her eyes searching his face, as though she was going to find something there to clarify his words, to explain why he'd spoken them at all.

"Love me? Oh, Laramie, are you sure you know what you're saying?"

A frown puckered his brow. "More sure than I've ever been about anything. Why? Don't you believe me?"

Her head swung gently back and forth. "Yes, I believe you. I'm just amazed, that's all. You could have any woman you want, Laramie. Especially one who doesn't have another man's child."

He groaned at her reasoning. "The fact that you are a mother makes you more lovable to me."

She looked at him through tear-filled eyes. "You're such a good man, Laramie. But loving me would mean taking on a heavy load. You could do better."

Sitting up at an angle to her back, he placed his hands on her bare shoulders and rested his cheek alongside hers. "It's hard for me to believe someone as beautiful and kind and precious as you has come into my life. And as far as me doing better—before you came to the ranch I'd given up on finding any woman to share my life. In case you hadn't noticed, I'm not exactly from a family of bluebloods. And I've sure never met a woman who would consider making a home with me here on the ranch, so many miles from civilization. But I happen to believe you're different—that you like it here. And that you can look past my lack of family. Most of all, I believe you care for me. More than you want to admit."

Bending her head, she sniffed and wiped at the moisture in her eyes. "I do care for you, Laramie. I—" Her words halted as her upper body suddenly twisted toward him and her hands desperately clutched his upper arms. "I more than care for you. I love you."

Just hearing her say the words sent joy spilling from his heart and spreading through him like warm rivulets of sunshine. Quickly, he gathered her into his arms and tried to convey all he was feeling in one lengthy kiss.

Finally, he eased his lips away from hers and spoke in a happy rush. "Oh, Leyla, darling. I want you to marry me. Soon! I want the three of us to be a family. And I don't want us to stop there. I want us to have more children. Children that will keep our love going on and on."

A wistful sigh passed her lips. "You make it sound so easy and wonderful."

He smiled. "It will be. All you have to do is say yes."

Her expression turned rueful. "You're asking me to take a huge step—to make all sorts of changes that would affect me and Dillon and my aunt."

"That's right," he said earnestly. "I'm asking. I'm hoping you love me enough to make those changes."

She turned her gaze away from him and over to the wide-paned window. Moonlight bathed her delicate profile, and as lovely as she looked at this moment, Laramie realized it was far more than her beauty that he'd fallen in love with. It was her gentle, caring essence and her quiet, sturdy strength.

"Oh, Laramie, I'm so honored that you feel this way. But my heart is tearing in all different directions right now."

He bent his head to press a kiss to her damp temple. "Why? If you love me, you shouldn't feel torn about anything."

Shifting toward him, she rested her head against his shoulder and Laramie took the opportunity to stroke the long hair lying against her back.

"Laramie, how can you be so sure about marriage? You're what—thirty-three or so? You've been a bachelor for a long time. You might decide that marriage wasn't what you want after all."

"I have been a bachelor for a long time. But that doesn't mean I'm confused. I've thought this out, Leyla, and I'm sure about what I want," he said firmly. "You're the one who clearly has doubts."

"We've not known each other that long. Being cautious makes sense," she countered.

Trying to stem his rising frustration, he closed his eyes, drew in a long breath, then heaved it out. "Does love always have to make sense? You deserve to give yourself a chance at happiness. To give Dillon—"

"You're right. I have Dillon to think of and—"

He interrupted her words by easing her head away from his shoulder. "And you want to find a man who can be a real daddy to Dillon, is that it? You don't believe a throwaway kid like me would ever be good enough to—"

"That's not what I'm thinking!"

Her evasive remark grated on his already bruised emotions. "Look, Leyla, I used to think I wasn't good enough to be a father. That because I didn't have a regular dad or come from a traditional family I wouldn't know how to be the sort of example a child needs, that I wouldn't know how to love or nurture or protect. But then I met you and Dillon and everything started to feel different to me. I began to dream and then I began to believe my life truly could be different." Taking her face between his palms, he gazed at her with firm conviction. "My mother and father walked out of my life and knowing the pain that's caused me—well, I could never walk away from Dillon or any other children we might be blessed enough to have."

Tears reappeared in her eyes and her throat worked as she swallowed hard. "I happen to think you'd make a great father."

"You do? Then what—"

Pulling away from him, she moved off the bed and plucked her robe from the floor. His mind whirling with confusion, he watched her slip her arms through the sleeves, then knot the sash at her waist.

"I have other responsibilities. Like Aunt Oneida. I'm all the family she has. Pretty soon she'll be well enough to get out of the nursing facility. She'll need a place to stay and me to care for her."

"We can deal with that."

"How? Move her into this house?" Tossing her hair back over her shoulders, she leveled a challenging look at him. "You can't just move a stranger in here, along with me and Dillon. Not on a permanent basis. You don't own this house."

The gist of her resistance suddenly dawned on him. He quickly slid from the bed and reached for his jeans. As he tugged them on, he tried to tamp down the anger and dejection that was threatening to overtake him.

"I see," he muttered, his voice a husky growl. "I get it now, Leyla. To you I'm just a glorified ranch hand and this house doesn't belong to me. My name isn't listed on the deed to the Chaparral. And that's all that's important to you, isn't it? Ownership!"

She gasped with outrage. "That's totally unfair. You don't understand. I—"

"I understand completely." Grabbing his shirt, he didn't bother putting it on. Instead he started toward the door. Once he opened it and stepped across the threshold, he paused and looked back at her. "I'm sorry, Leyla. I'm the one who's made a mistake. I believed you and I were on the same page. Today in the little stucco I thought—" He shook his head with rueful acceptance. "Forget it. Forget everything."

The next morning, as Leyla sat at the kitchen table, her hands clutched tightly around a mug of coffee, she wondered why she'd even bothered to go to bed last night after Laramie had left so abruptly. She'd not slept at all. Instead, she'd lain awake staring at the ceiling and asking herself why she was so weak, so willing to follow a path to heartache.

The sound of Dillon's bare feet rapidly pattering into the kitchen brought her head around and she forced a bright smile as he ran the last few steps to her.

"Good morning, sweet face." Drawing him close, she pecked kisses on both his cheeks.

Giggling, he wiped at the spots with one fist. "Me not sweet face, Mommy. Me cowboy."

Sighing, she rose to her feet and walked over to the cabinets. "And a very cute one," she told her son. "Are you ready for breakfast, cowboy?"

"I wanna get my boots and hat. I wanna wear 'em now. So Larmee can see me."

He started to turn and race out of the room, but Leyla quickly called out to him.

"Wait, Dillon. Laramie isn't going to eat breakfast with us this morning. He's already gone. He had to eat early and go to work." At least that's what the brief note had stated. The one she'd found pinned to the refrigerator when she'd entered the kitchen earlier this morning. It was possible that he'd truly had to leave the house before daylight. It certainly wouldn't be the first time such a thing had happened. But in this incidence Leyla figured he'd used work as an excuse not to see her. The notion just piled on more hurt to the pain and regret she'd already been feeling.

Moping now, Dillon went over to the table and climbed onto one of the chairs. With his chin resting against his chest, he remained silent. Her son's disappointment now was only just the beginning of how it would be once the two of them left the ranch and the man was truly out of their lives.

Walking over to him, Leyla gave his shoulders an affectionate squeeze. "You can still wear your boots and hat if you want to," she suggested.

His head wagged back and forth, the dejected movement accompanied by a telltale sniff. Leyla used her forefinger to lift his face up toward hers. "What's this?" she asked, speaking of his tears. "Don't you remember what Laramie told you? Cowboys don't cry."

Nodding, he scrubbed his eyes with both fists, then asked with eager anticipation, "Will Larmee come home tonight?"

Her chest tight with pain, she did her best to give him an encouraging smile. "I'm sure he will. And I'm sure he'll want to see you."

If Laramie allowed the rift between them to keep him away from Dillon, then he wasn't nearly the man she'd thought him to be.

Later that morning, Sassy arrived for work and Leyla was braced for more questions and innuendoes regarding Laramie. But the other woman surprised her by not mentioning him at all. Leyla was grateful. She wasn't in the mood to deal with Sassy's well-meaning advice.

Instead, when the two women stopped for lunch, Sassy brought up the subject of Reena and the question of when she'd be returning to the Chaparral.

"You haven't heard from her today, have you?" Sassy asked as she folded a piece of bologna between a piece of bread.

Across the kitchen table, Leyla had been forcing herself to eat a small portion of tuna salad. "Why no," Leyla replied. "Did she say she was going to call back?"

"Not exactly. But I got the impression she would. If I remember right, Jim's checkup was this morning. Why don't you call her? She might have some news about his X-rays."

It would certainly help to know how many more days she could expect to be here, Leyla thought. But she didn't like the idea of calling the woman and pressing her for information.

"I don't think I should. She might get the wrong idea."

Making an impatient sound, Sassy swallowed the last of the bologna and bread and rose to her feet. "Don't be ridiculous. She won't think anything of it. I'll call her myself."

Picking up the phone on the end of the cabinet, Sassy made the call. While her friend talked, Leyla tried not to listen to the one-sided conversation. Instead, she turned her attention to Dillon, who was making a game of crumbling crackers into his alphabet soup.

After a somewhat lengthy swap of words, Sassy finally placed the receiver back on its hook and walked back to the table. Leyla took one glance at the puckered frown on the other woman's face and wondered what could have possibly put it there.

"Jim's X-rays were good. The bone is healed. The cast is off and he's starting therapy tomorrow," she relayed.

Leyla didn't know whether to cry or shout with joy. Common sense told her that the quicker she left this ranch and put distance between herself and Laramie, the better off she'd be. But her heart wasn't listening to logic. She loved Laramie. To leave him would be like tearing out her heart and tossing it away.

"Oh. That's good news," she said.

Sassy seemed unaware of the guarded note in Leyla's voice. Instead, she reached for a potato chip. "I asked Reena when she thought she'd be coming home. But she didn't make much sense when she answered."

Trying not to appear anxious, Leyla asked, "What do you mean?"

Sassy shrugged. "I'm not sure. She started talking about how much Abe needed her there and that she wasn't about to leave him just yet. Along with that I got the feeling that she wasn't looking forward to leaving the old man period." She looked at Leyla and let out a short, incredulous laugh. "Wouldn't that be something? Reena and Abe. Who would have ever thought it?"

"Well, the last time I talked with her," Leyla said, "I recall her calling him a sweetheart. But I thought she meant it in a general sense." She glanced at Sassy. "There's a large age gap between the two of them, isn't there? I've not met the elder Cantrell, but his photo is on the desk in the study. He looks somewhat older than Reena."

Sassy laughed. "Somewhat! Honey, I'd guess Abe has to be around eighty-six, if he's a day. But to be fair, he gets around like a man thirty years younger." A wistful expression came over the maid's face as she gazed beyond Leyla's shoulder to the window overlooking the ranch yard. "Isn't it romantic? Reena is such a lovely woman and she's been alone for so long. To think she's fallen for Abe—well, it's just dreamy."

"It's surprising," Leyla replied.

Annoyed with Leyla's attitude, Sassy glanced at her. "Leyla, you're just not a romantic soul. And I can hardly figure why when you obviously have Laramie wrapped around your little finger."

Rising quickly to her feet, Leyla carried her dirty dish to the sink. " I don't want to talk about him," she said firmly.

A long stretch of silence passed and then Sassy said, "Well, at least you don't have to worry about leaving the ranch anytime soon, if ever. Because frankly, I don't believe Reena intends to come back to the Chaparral."

How would that change things for her and Dillon? Leyla wondered, her mind spinning in all directions. Laramie had asked her to marry him. Most any woman in her shoes would be walking on a cloud about now. Instead, she was frozen with doubts and fears.

When she'd told him that she loved him, the words had come straight from her heart. But for them to be married—how would it ever work? She'd definitely have to forsake her plans to be a nurse. At least, for a while. Along with that he'd be taking on more than a wife. Dillon and Oneida would also become his responsibilities. That was a lot to ask a man who'd been a bachelor all his life. What if the stress of it all crushed his love for her? Or should she be giving him more credit? He'd dealt with all sorts of heavy loads in his life. Maybe he could handle a ready-made family.

Forget the questions, Leyla. You've probably already managed to kill whatever feelings Laramie had for you. He believes you have your sights on bigger fish. He thinks you're all about owning. Not loving.

Oh, God, what was she going to do? she silently prayed.

"Leyla, is anything wrong?"

Sassy's voice penetrated her thoughts and she glanced

over to see the maid had gotten to her feet and was now approaching her.

"No. I was just thinking about things." She did her best to smile. "I think I'd better go check on my aunt tomorrow. Would you like to drive into town with me?"

"Sure. We'll stop by the Blue Mesa and I'll buy Dillon a big ice cream cone and we'll have pie."

Leyla rolled her eyes. "Do you ever stop thinking of dessert?"

Sassy laughed. "Only when I'm thinking about a man."

Dusk was approaching later that evening when Laramie braked his truck to a halt at the back of the house. As soon as he stepped through the gate, he spotted Dillon rolling in the grass with his kittens, Cookie and Stripes.

Unaware that a wistful expression had softened his hard features, Laramie paused to take in the sight. No matter what had occurred with him and Leyla, the boy already felt like his son. If she took him away, it would be like tearing off Laramie's arm or leg. He'd survive, but it would be damned hard.

After a moment, the child spotted him standing on the stone walkway and Laramie felt a sense of utter love as Dillon raced to greet him.

"Larmee! Larmee!"

Chuckling, he swung Dillon up in his arms. "How's my partner?"

Grinning broadly, the child hooked an arm around Laramie's neck. "I'm good! See my boots? Mommy let me wear 'em. I can't get 'em dirty, though. She be mad."

Laramie made a show of inspecting Dillon's boots. "I think she'll be happy. They look pretty clean to me."

Laramie wanted to tell the child that cowboy boots were made for getting dirty. But he had no right to go against

Leyla's instructions to her son. No doubt she would resent it. The way she'd resented his marriage proposal, he thought grimly.

He'd tried all day to forget the list of reasons she had for not marrying him, to forget the emptiness he'd felt when he'd left her apartment last night. But nothing, not even hours in the saddle or dealing with a broken windmill and a herd of thirsty cattle, had been able to push the miserable thoughts from his mind.

He didn't want to lose her. He loved her. More than he'd ever imagined he could love anyone. Was he crazy or just too damned weak to care that she wanted to own a house more than she wanted to be with him? He'd asked himself that question all day. And the more he'd thought, the more he'd decided that Leyla's reaction to his proposal had nothing to do with a house, or Dillon, or her ailing aunt. It was everything to do with trust. Of taking a chance on him and all the things that could bring her happiness.

That's why he couldn't say to hell with his plans with her. He couldn't turn his back and forget all the pleasure and wonderful dreams she'd brought to his life. He had to find some way to open her eyes, to show her what really mattered to the both of them.

Stepping into the atrium, with Dillon still riding the crook of his arm, he asked, "Is Mommy cooking?"

"She cookin'," the youngster answered. "You gonna eat, too, Larmee?"

Laramie hugged the child a little tighter. "I sure am. We're going to eat together."

Inside the kitchen his gaze quickly searched the room until it landed on Leyla. As yet unaware of their presence, he watched as she methodically placed plates and silverware on the table. Wearing a black-and-white gingham dress that swished against her knees and with her long hair in a braid swept to one side of her head, she looked dainty and feminine. Her beauty always jolted him, but now that he'd explored the wonders of her body, now that he knew what pleasures waited in her arms, the sight of her hit him especially hard.

Swallowing at the tightness in his throat, he lowered Dillon to the floor. The boy quickly raced to his mother's side.

"Larmee gonna eat, too, Mommy! See! Larmee home!"

Pausing in her task, she followed the direction of Dillon's pointing finger. When her gaze caught sight of Laramie, her lips parted with surprise, but that was the only expression he could read on her face.

As he moved toward her, she spoke in a guarded tone, "Oh. I didn't expect you to be here. I'll get another plate."

"Sorry," he said stiffly. "I should've let you know I'd be coming in at a normal hour. But the way my schedule has been here lately I never know where I'll be or when."

Leaving the table, she walked over to the cabinets. Laramie crossed to where she stood with Dillon following close on his heels.

Pulling a plate from the cabinet, she said, "I found your note this morning."

Even though he'd left her apartment in a turmoil last night, he'd not been trying to evade her. Giving her the cold shoulder this morning wouldn't have solved anything. It would only prove he was hardly capable of being a husband or family man.

"A late calving heifer was having a problem giving birth. I went down to the vet barn to assist Russ. With Laurel pregnant it's not good for her to do any heavy straining and the hands have all been working so hard, I didn't want to get one of them out of bed when I could help instead. Turned out the heifer had to have a C-section."

Her expression sheepish, Leyla turned to face him. "I...I thought—well, that you'd probably gone to the bunkhouse to eat."

"I'm sorry you didn't believe my note."

Her guilty gaze slipped to a grinning Dillon. Thankfully the child appeared to be totally unaware of the stiff tension between Laramie and his mother.

"Well, you were upset with me last night," she explained.

"Disappointed is a better word."

With a nervous lick of her lips, she looked at him and he was struck by the confusion and hurt on her face. At that moment, Laramie wanted to pull her into his arms. He wanted to tell her that there was no need for either of them to suffer and that somehow they could make it work.

"Laramie, I need for you to understand."

With Dillon wedged between their legs and listening to every word they were exchanging, he was forced to limit his reply. "I think I do," he said huskily, then reached down for Dillon's hand. "Come on, saddle pal. Let's me and you go wash up."

During supper Leyla was very quiet, but Dillon made up for his mother's lack of conversation with his endless chatter. During the past few weeks, Laramie had watched the child's self-confidence grow in leaps and bounds. There was no doubt that his surroundings had helped Dillon to thrive and grow from that quiet and shy youngster who'd first arrived here on the Chaparral. But had Leyla noticed just how much the ranch was doing for her son? And if she had, did it really matter to her?

Giving Dillon a daddy didn't appear to be on the top of her want list, Laramie thought dourly. Compared to buying a house for the kid to live in, it didn't even make her priority list.

You're not being totally fair, Laramie. You've never been homeless or lived in a run-down structure that lacked the most basic facilities. If you had, you might understand where Leyla's coming from. And it's not just a house she wants. She has dreams to become a nurse and make something more of herself.

I need for you to understand.

There'd been a beseeching sound in her voice when she'd spoken those words to him, and it suddenly dawned on Laramie that for the past few years fear had been the catalyst pushing Leyla forward, the thing that had shaped and directed every choice she'd made concerning her and Dillon's life and future.

So how was he going to change that? Laramie wondered. He didn't know. He only knew that somehow, someway, he had to help her put her fears aside once and for all. Otherwise, the three of them could never have a future together.

Chapter Twelve

The three of them had just finished the meal and Leyla was making coffee to go with the dessert when he was called once again to the vet barn. This time the emergency involved a crippled horse, and Laramie remained there until Russ had taken X-rays and determined the horse would survive.

By the time he finally returned to the ranch house, the evening had grown late and Leyla had already retired to her apartment.

She answered his knock almost immediately, and as he followed her into the cozy living room, he removed his hat and combed a hand through his hair.

"I was about to decide you weren't coming back anytime soon," she said, then gestured for him to take a seat.

"Has Dillon already gone to bed?" As he sat on one end of the couch, he noticed several textbooks lying on the coffee table. Next to them was a legal pad with a page full of notes. Clearly she'd not dismissed her plans to become a nurse, he thought. But then he'd never expected or wanted her to simply drop her dreams because he'd asked her to marry him. He should have made that more clear to her, he thought. He should have assured her that he would never be a controlling or demanding husband.

"He tried to stay awake," she said as she sank onto the cushion next to him. "But I finally put him to bed about an hour ago."

"It took a while for Russ to do X-rays and make a diagnosis. I wanted to hang around to see if the horse was going to be okay or would have to be put down."

"Will it be all right?" she asked with obvious concern.

"Russ is performing surgery right now to remove a bone chip in his knee. He'll be fine after a long rest."

"So it wasn't something caused by one of those mysterious accidents?"

"No, thank God," he answered. "Just a work injury out on the range."

Her sigh was full of relief. "That's good," she said, then after nervously rubbing her hands down the skirt of her dress, she suddenly rose to her feet. "I have coffee in the kitchen. I'll get you a cup."

His hand shot out and caught her wrist before she could move away. "No. Maccoy made a pot in Russ's office. I drank some there. Besides, I want us to talk before something else interrupts us."

She slowly eased back onto the couch. "I'm not sure there's anything else left for us to say, Laramie. I've been thinking and—"

"That's just it," he interrupted, "you've been thinking too much with your head instead of your heart."

She closed her eyes and, as he watched her swallow, it

was clear she was torn and confused. Maybe she wasn't even sure that she loved him.

Hell, Laramie, if she really loved you, nothing else would matter. Not a house or property. Not her ailing aunt or anything else. She'd wrap her arms around you and never let go. And if you loved her you'd let her know that this ranch and your job mean nothing compared to having her in your life.

Releasing his hold on her wrist, he went on, "And I'm beginning to think I've asked too much of you. I've expected you to do all the sacrificing. I've been thinking about everything I want when I should've been listening more to what you want."

She stared at him in wonder. "What do you mean?"

As he gazed at her lovely face, everything inside him wanted to pull her into his arms and make love to her, but his head was telling him that taking her to bed wouldn't fix anything.

"I'm trying to tell you, Leyla, that if living here on the ranch is that much of a problem for you, then I'll leave it behind."

Her lips parted with disbelief. "Leave the ranch," she echoed in a stunned voice. "Laramie, that's not a solution. It's crazy!"

"There's nothing crazy in wanting us to be together," he gently reasoned.

She swallowed hard and pain skewered the middle of his chest as he watched moisture flood her brown eyes.

"No. But the idea of you leaving this ranch is. The Chaparral is your home. Where would you go? What would you do?"

"We could move to Las Cruces or Albuquerque. Some city where you can become an RN."

Her head moved ever so slightly back and forth. "But

what would you do in a city? You'd be stifled and unhappy," she argued.

"There would be ranches in the nearby countryside. I could take a job on one of them and commute back and forth to work," he reasoned. "What would be wrong with that?"

She jumped to her feet as though she desperately needed to put space between them. By the time she reached the far end of the room, Laramie was standing in front of her, cutting off her path to nowhere.

"Answer me, Leyla," he challenged.

Lifting her chin, she met his gaze. "Okay. You want an answer, so I'll tell you. Everything would be wrong with it," she said in a strained voice. "You and I both know that to manage a ranch you have to be on that ranch."

He heaved out a heavy breath. "Well, I don't have to work as a manager. I—"

"No!" she swiftly interrupted. "You're not going to lower yourself to working as a day hand! Not any more than I would let you give up your home. Do you honestly think I could be happy knowing that you gave up everything just to please me?"

Sheer frustration pulled a groan from deep within him. "I don't know what you want or expect from me, Leyla. You don't want me here. You don't want me there. Maybe that's it. Maybe you just don't want me as your husband under any circumstances."

A tiny sob passed her lips and she lifted her hands to cover her face but not before he saw her features crumple with anguish. "That's not true. I love you. I would love to be your wife." Dropping her hands, she looked up at him. "But I'm afraid, Laramie. Nothing has ever lasted for me. And you loving me seems just too good to be true—too good to last."

His hands settled on her shoulders. "Oh, Leyla, good things can happen to you. All you have to do is let them and believe that we can make it together."

Tears continued to cloud her eyes. "My mother always told me and my sisters that we shouldn't expect to have a wonderful life. She said that we needed to be realistic and remember our limitations and settle for comfortable."

Laramie didn't understand how he could feel sadness for Mrs. Chee. He'd never met the woman. Never even seen a picture of her. But clearly she was a woman who'd been used and had passed her failings and weaknesses on to her daughters. Perhaps his own mother had been in that same category, he thought. Maybe Peggy had run from him and her life in Lincoln County because no one had ever told her she could do better, be better. It was a sobering thought.

"She wants her daughters to be like her," Laramie softly stated.

Nodding, Leyla dropped her head. "My mother has always been too weak to stand up for herself. And I don't want to be like her. I do have pride and I don't intend to let anyone squash me like my father has stomped my mother."

He shook his head. "Leyla, I wouldn't use marriage to take away your independence. You can still be a nurse or whatever you want to be. Just as long as we're together."

Her head lifted and her eyes were full of torment. "Sassy spoke to Reena this morning. Jim's cast is off and he's starting therapy. She doesn't believe Reena will be coming back here to the ranch anytime soon. But I do."

Quint hadn't mentioned this news about Jim to Laramie, and hearing it now hit him in the gut. He had to convince Leyla to marry him soon; otherwise, he was certain that if she left the ranch, he would lose her forever.

Studying her closely, he asked in a strained voice, "Is that what you want? To go back to the reservation?"

Her eyes blinked as though his question had jolted her awake. "No. But I'm thinking it might be best."

Lifting one hand from her shoulders, he touched her hair, then trailed his fingertips over her cheek and underneath her jaw. "Why?"

Her hands rested on his chest, then slid slowly, wantonly up to where his shirt parted and her fingers could touch his bared skin. "Because when you're near me, I can't think straight. Because all I want to do is make love to you. To say yes to anything you want."

The war inside him was raging now as the choice to pick her up and carry her to the bedroom battled with his plans for their future.

Catching her hands, he pressed them firmly between his. "You don't have to worry about that, Leyla."

Her brows drew together. "You mean you don't want us to—"

She couldn't finish the words and Laramie spared her by swiftly bending his head and fastening a hot, hungry kiss on her lips. "Hell, yes, I want us to make love!" he muttered once he eased his mouth from hers. "But not like this. The next time I take you to bed, it will be as my wife or I won't take you at all."

Anger suddenly flared in her eyes, and in his arms he could feel her body stiffen. "What are you doing? Trying to blackmail me into marrying you by withholding sex? What kind of arrogant bastard are you?"

She flung the questions at him at the same time she twisted out of his embrace. Laramie reacted by catching her wrist and drawing her back to him.

"Blackmail, coercing, forcing. None of those things have anything to do with this," he said gruffly. "Earlier you told me you had pride. Well, so do I, Leyla. And men are no different than women. They don't want to be used."

She gasped and from the expression in her eyes, he could see her mind was whirling with thoughts she'd never encountered before.

"Using you? I would never use you, Laramie! How could you think such a thing?"

With a muffled groan, he caught her by the shoulders and tugged her back into his arms. "Listen, Leyla, yesterday I wasn't just having sex with you. I was giving you a part of my heart. I can't keep giving that much of myself to you if you're just going to walk away and take everything with you. I like to believe I'm a strong man, but I'm not that strong."

He dropped a kiss on her forehead, then for a second time in two nights, he strode purposely out of the apartment.

The next week passed in a tortured daze for Leyla. Even though Laramie treated her with polite respect, nothing felt the same between them. And she doubted their relationship could ever go back to the way it had felt that wonderful day they'd made love in the stucco.

When she'd told him she was afraid, she'd been admitting her fears to herself just as much as she'd been confessing it to him. But admitting it hadn't taken the fears away or given her the courage to go to Laramie and tell him she was ready to be his wife.

But why was she still afraid? Laramie was willing to give up his job and this beautiful home just for her. That alone proved he loved her very much. Wasn't it time she proved that she loved him just as much?

Four days ago she'd gone to visit her aunt Oneida, and though she'd desperately wanted to talk with the older woman about her feelings for Laramie and his proposal of marriage, Leyla had kept it all to herself. She didn't want the woman worrying for any reason. And she especially didn't want Oneida to fret that her niece was going to get married and forget her.

Other than Oneida, Leyla had no family to confide in. Oh, if she really wanted, she could get in touch with her mother. But if her father found out, he'd only cause Juanita Chee more grief. She had her sister Zita's phone number, too. But ever since Leyla had left home, Zita hadn't made much effort to remain in close contact with her younger sister. In fact, the few times she had talked with Zita, she'd gotten the impression she blamed Leyla for their mother's misery. And that hurt. For as long as she could remember, Juanita had been miserable. Leyla getting pregnant and leaving home had just been one of many disappointments Juanita had endured in her life.

But that was in the past, and for four years she'd been strong enough to care for herself and Dillon. She was strong enough to make a life with Laramie and deal with the complications that came with having a family. But would he believe that she'd finally recognized what their love for each other meant to her? She'd been so obstinate he might have already decided she wasn't worth the trouble.

"Mommy, let's go see Tommy. He wants to see us."

At the sound of her son's voice, Leyla glanced up from the cabbage she was chopping to see Dillon standing in the middle of the kitchen floor. The day was very warm, so she'd dressed him in shorts and a T-shirt, but he'd insisted on wearing his boots and hat. For the past fifteen minutes he'd been riding a broom around the room.

"I'm busy right now," she told him. Leyla had long ago given up on convincing her son that the cat in the vet barn wasn't Tommy. She'd actually decided it was probably easier on him to believe his first pet was still living close by. "And Tommy is probably out hunting a mouse to feed to his kittens."

Dillon tilted his head to one side. "Then we see Cocoa. I wanna give him a carrot and ride him."

"Laramie has to be with you whenever you ride Cocoa. And he's at work."

Dillon galloped his make-believe horse over to his mother. "Let's go find Larmee. He let me ride Cocoa."

Yes, she thought, her heart swelling with emotion, Laramie had patiently and lovingly allowed Dillon to do so many special things. He'd changed her son's life and, along the way, he'd changed Leyla's life, too. Waiting to tell him how she felt about him was senseless when her heart was telling her to run to him as fast as her legs could take her.

Dropping her knife onto the cutting board, she looked down at her son. "Okay, Dillon, let Mommy change her shoes and we'll go find Laramie."

Dillon was squealing with joy just as Sassy hurried into the kitchen with an odd look on her pale face.

"Leyla, there's someone out on the front porch who wants to see you. I tried to get him to come into the house, but he refused."

Sensing that something was amiss, Leyla's heart kicked to high gear. "He? What's his name?"

"Tanno or something like that? Do you know him, or should I send him away?"

Shock caused Leyla to grip the edge of the counter. *What had happened to send Tanno here? Had someone in her family been hurt or, God forbid, died?* "Yes. I know him. He's my brother."

With dazed movements, she wiped her hands on a dish towel, then headed to the front of the house.

* * *

A few years back, Quint had built a separate building to house a staff of secretaries and filing clerks to deal with all the paperwork required to keep a ranch of this magnitude going. As a result Laramie rarely had to deal with paperwork, and his office, which was located at one end of the horse barn, was rarely used, except to meet certain visitors or carry on a private, sit-down phone call.

As the owner of the ranch, Quint certainly didn't regard himself as a visitor, but after a quick look around the ranch this afternoon, he'd herded Laramie into the dusty little office and ordered him to sit.

"Why don't we go to the house and talk in the study?" Laramie suggested. "I'm sure Leyla would make coffee and she always has some kind of dessert sitting around."

"Forget that. She's the reason I wanted to talk to you out here. I don't want to take a chance on her overhearing us."

Suspicious now, Laramie eased down in a chair that afforded him a view to the east. If not for a long feed barn standing in the way, he could have seen the rear of the ranch house and the fenced backyard where Dillon often played.

"Why would you want to talk about Leyla? Has she done something wrong? Gone over her grocery budget?"

"Not hardly. She doesn't even use what we allot her for each week. What does she feed you anyway—bologna or ramen noodles?"

"No! She cooks wonderful things." He patted his flat midsection. "I'm surprised I haven't gained weight."

Quint leveled a serious look at him. "Well, I don't have any complaints about the job Leyla's doing."

Laramie's mind began to go in all sorts of directions. "Then you're wanting to tell me about Jim. But Leyla's already told me that he got his cast off. So Reena must be packing to come home. Is that it?"

Rolling his eyes toward the ceiling, Quint shook his head. "Quite the contrary. I don't think Reena will ever return here to the Chaparral. At least, not as cook."

Caught by Quint's remark, Laramie leaned toward the other man. "What the hell is the matter with Reena? This has been her home for longer than I've been alive."

"Nothing is wrong. Except that she's in love with my grandfather and he with her."

Stunned, Laramie stared at the man who was his boss and also like his brother. "Are you kidding me?"

Quint shook his head. "Not hardly."

"But Reena and Abe have known each other for many years! Why now? All of a sudden?"

Shrugging, Quint said, "Maura believes it's because this is the first time they've ever been thrown together in the same house for an extended length of time. I guess it gave them the chance to—well, grow close. Hell, we both know how much Abe loves women. If he'd not been so chained to Grandmother's ghost, he would have probably remarried years ago. Reena is a lovely woman. And Grandfather—"

"Is a charmer," Laramie finished for him. "Is this romance of theirs bothering you? Is that why you're telling me?"

With his hat resting in his lap, Quint raked both hands through his hair. "At first I was worried, but I can see how happy he is." His gaze settled back on Laramie's face. "I'm telling you all this because I expect them to get married and—"

"Married! Abe?"

"What the hell am I talking for?" Quint impatiently barked the question. "Apparently you aren't listening."

"I hear you. But I thought this was all about them just having a romance—a relationship."

Quint scowled at him. "Grandfather is an honorable man. And so are you."

Quint's remark had Laramie gaping at him. "Me? What are you bringing me up for?"

"Because I think you're in love with Leyla. And this change in Reena's plans will ultimately affect her. Do you think she'll stay on? Have you asked her?"

A sick feeling swam in Laramie's stomach, and from the way Quint was looking at him, he figured his swarthy skin must have gone pale. "I've asked her to marry me. But she's pretty much turned me down. I—"

Laramie's words were halted by a loud knock on the door followed by Sassy's gasping voice.

"Laramie? Are you in there?"

Before either man could open the door, the maid jerked it open and burst into the room.

Quint, nearest to the door, jumped to his feet and grabbed her arm to steady her. "Sassy! What's going on?"

She looked frantically to Laramie. Sensing the worse, he quickly shot to his feet.

"You need to come to the house! Quick!"

"What's wrong?" Laramie demanded.

"Has someone been hurt?" Quint added.

The violent shake of Sassy's head sent her red curls flying. "No. Not hurt. But I'm afraid that something is going to happen. Leyla's brother is here. I'm afraid he's going to force her and Dillon to leave with him! I overheard him telling Leyla to go pack her bags. Hurry! You've got to get to the house and stop them!" she pleaded.

Leyla's brother! Except for her aunt and her sisters, Laramie didn't think she'd been in contact with any of her family for a long time. In fact, the few remarks she'd made about her brother hadn't exactly been complimentary. He couldn't imagine her inviting him to the ranch. What would her brother be doing here?

"Don't panic, Sassy," he said to the maid, then looked over to Quint. "I gotta go."

At the house, Leyla stood facing her brother and wondered why the urge to laugh kept running through her like the intermittent volt of an electric line. There was nothing funny about Tanno arriving on the ranch and ordering her to go pack her bags. And it was hardly amusing to hear that her father now claimed he'd forgiven her and wanted her to come home. They both knew that the only reason George Chee would want her back in the house was to work and help pay the bills while he made excuses to stay home and drink beer.

"How did you know where to find me?" Leyla asked while Dillon stood silently at her side, clutching the folds of her skirt.

The tall young man with dark brown hair and chiseled features stared impatiently at his sister and nephew. Tanno had never been judgmental of Leyla. But he'd also never been supportive. He mostly kept to himself and tried to avoid riling their father's temper. She supposed he was here today only because George had forced him to make the trip.

"Mom called Aunt Oneida and asked her," he answered. "Why? Were you trying to keep your whereabouts a secret?"

On the reservation, Oneida hadn't had telephone service of any kind. But there was a telephone in Oneida's room in the nursing home.

"No. It doesn't matter. It's not like I've been smothered

with doting, concerned family these past few years," she said dryly.

In defense of the Chee family, Tanno said, "We all thought of you and wondered how you were doing. Especially Mom."

Leyla suddenly felt very sad. Not for herself, but for her mother. Leyla had somehow found the courage to move on. Juanita never would. "Yes," Leyla said mockingly, "she was wondering so much she traveled down here to her daughter and only grandchild to make sure we were okay."

Clearly stunned by her outspokenness, Tanno stared at her. Leyla suddenly realized just how much she'd changed, how different a person she was compared to the frightened girl who had climbed onto a bus in Farmington with little more than a small duffel bag filled with personal items and a few dollars in her pocket.

"None of that matters anymore," Tanno said. "Dad wants you home now. You will be welcome. Everything will be as it used to be."

Groaning with frustration, she said, "Oh, Tanno, why would I want to go back to the way it used to be? Why can't you just speak the truth of the matter? Dad wants money, doesn't he? He wants me home so that he can order me to hand over my wages to him."

A shamed look came over his face. "Well, he can't pay the bills. And Mom can't keep up. I try to help, but I'm saving to go to college. Zita and Tawnee moved out a few weeks ago. They rented an apartment together in town."

"Oh, I see now. Income has gone down in the Chee household so Dad sent you to drag me back home."

Tanno appeared totally bewildered. "Dad will always be the same, Leyla. I thought you'd want to come home for Mom's sake."

As Leyla faced her brother it dawned on her that she

couldn't expect her brother to see things as she could now. Since she'd left her home on the Navajo reservation, she'd had to fight to survive. And during that battle, she'd changed and learned and matured into a woman. She was so different from the girl who'd once made a bad choice. She was strong. She was capable. And from this day forward she was never going to look back.

"Mom is a good woman and I love her very much. But I can't live my life to pay for her mistakes or Dad's laziness. I won't be going back to the res with you."

Her brother scrubbed a hand over his face as though to wake himself from a dream. "But what will I tell the family? Do you plan to ever see them again?"

She let out a long breath as everything inside her came together and settled peacefully in the middle of her heart. "I will bring Dillon up for a visit soon and let them see their grandchild. From there, I'll have to see how things go," she told him. "But as for mine and Dillon's future, I'm getting married to a man I love very much and our home will always be here on the Chaparral with him."

"Leyla!"

The sound of Laramie's voice had Leyla spinning around to see him striding quickly toward her and Dillon. And the look of amazement on his face told her he'd overheard the last few words she'd spoken to Tanno. What was he thinking, feeling? she wondered. Was he going to tell Tanno that the wedding was off? That she'd waited too long to come to her senses?

Her heart was racing so badly she could hardly speak. "Laramie! What are you doing here?"

By now he'd reached her side, but before he could answer her question Dillon let out a whoop of joy and latched a possessive hold on Laramie's leg.

With a protective hand on Dillon's head, he glanced at

Leyla, then settled a curious gaze on Tanno. "Sassy came to my office and told me you had company. I thought you might want me to meet him."

Leyla stiffly inclined her head toward her brother. "Laramie, this is my brother, Tanno Chee."

Laramie extended a hand to the younger man. "Laramie Jones," he introduced himself. "Nice to meet you."

Leyla could see that the sight of Laramie had knocked Tanno for a loop, which made her wonder if her brother had doubted her talk about getting married.

As he shook Laramie's hand, he asked, "Are you the man my sister is going to marry?"

Laramie's gaze settled on Leyla's face and the look she saw in his eyes filled her heart with such joy that tears stung her eyes.

"I am," he said.

Clearly bewildered, Tanno asked, "And you live here? At this house?"

"That's right. I'm the manager of this ranch."

Tanno looked at his sister, then back to Laramie as though he didn't know what to say or think. At that moment Leyla realized how much she loved her brother and how much she hoped his life would soon change for the better.

"So you won't need to worry about your sister, Mr. Chee. I plan to take very good care of her."

As he said the last words his arm came around the back of her waist and she smiled up at him, her heart overflowing with happiness. "And Dillon and I are planning to be very happy," she added.

With his fingers tightening on her side, Laramie glanced at the other man. "Would you like to come in?" he invited. "You probably need a break. We'll have refreshments and you can get acquainted with your nephew."

Tanno's focus dropped to Dillon, and Leyla could see a wistful sort of smile briefly touch her brother's lips. "Thank you, Mr. Jones. Maybe next time."

"I hope there will be a next time, Tanno. Leyla and I will always welcome you here. Please remember that."

Tanno nodded awkwardly. "I'll remember. Right now I'd better be going."

Her throat tight with emotion, Leyla stepped forward and placed a kiss on her brother's cheek. They'd never been a physically affectionate family, so her act caught him completely off-guard, but she hoped that as he traveled back to the reservation he would think about it and everything she'd said to him.

"Goodbye, Tanno."

Tanno gave them all one last glance before he left the porch and climbed into his old truck. It wasn't until they'd waved him off that Laramie turned his complete attention to Leyla.

"You did really mean that, didn't you? When you told Tanno you were going to marry me and make your home here?"

Moving closer, she slipped her arms around his waist. "Every word," she murmured.

His gentle gaze slipped over her face. "What made you change your mind? Seeing Tanno?"

She lifted fingers to his cheek. "No. Believe it or not, just before he showed up I was about to come find you and tell you that I've been foolish and miserable. You offered to give up everything for me, Laramie. I can give up everything for you, too. Because I love you."

Bending his head he gave her a kiss full of promises. "You'll see, Leyla. We're not going to give up anything. We're going to gain everything."

Apparently tired of waiting on the adults to take notice

of him, Dillon suddenly began to tug on the leg of Laramie's jeans. "Larmee! Larmee! I wanna go ride Cocoa!"

Leyla and Laramie looked down at him and began to laugh.

"Just wait until we have two or three more children to go with Dillon," Leyla warned with a smile. "You'll need a whole string of ponies to keep them all happy."

Love put a husky note to his voice. "I can't wait," he said, then with his arm around Leyla's waist and his hand wrapped firmly on Dillon's shoulder, Laramie guided his family into their home.

Epilogue

A month later, Laramie and Leyla were married in a simple but beautiful ceremony in the same little church where Diego had taken baby Laramie to be christened and, later as a child, to worship. Afterward, they'd celebrated with an outdoor reception at the Chaparral. All the ranch hands, along with friends and neighbors, had attended. On that special day, Leyla had truly felt as though she had become a part of the Chaparral.

Six weeks had passed since their wedding and during that time Oneida had been released from the nursing home. Leyla and Dillon had moved into the big house with Laramie, so they'd decided Reena's vacant suite would be perfect to give Oneida privacy yet still be close to her family if she needed help.

So far the older woman was thriving and had grown adept at using a walker to maneuver herself from room to room. She loved living in the country and under the same roof as her niece. Especially because the roof didn't leak, she often joked.

As for Leyla's family back on the Navajo reservation, she'd been shocked a few weeks ago when her mother had called to congratulate her on her wedding. Not only that, her sisters Tawnee and Zita had come by for a long visit. All in all Leyla was feeling more encouraged about building a relationship with her relatives again, and as soon as Laramie found a free day they were planning on driving up to see her parents. She wasn't naive enough to expect her father to have suddenly changed, but she wanted to try to develop some sort of connection with the man. And who knew, maybe now that George's children were leaving the nest, his eyes would open up to his shortcomings.

Loving Laramie and becoming his wife had Leyla looking to the future with different eyes. Before she'd agreed to marry him, she'd been locked on plans to become a registered nurse, but now she realized she didn't want to be away from her husband or son for the length of time it would take to acquire such a degree. Especially because they wanted to have more children. So in the meantime, she'd come up with a solution that would still allow her to be a nurse but also be with her family. In a matter of weeks she would be enrolling in a short-term training course in nearby Ruidoso to become a practical nurse. Once she was finished she could use her skills to treat home health patients, like her aunt Oneida, and keep her work hours to a minimum.

Suddenly aware of an arm tightening around the back of her waist, Leyla glanced over her shoulder to see her husband had joined her at a long table laden with an array of rich, delicious foods.

"Coming back for seconds?" he teased.

Tonight, a party was taking place in the big ranch house;

however, this time the social gathering had nothing to do with Leyla and Laramie; the Cantrells and their friends had gathered to celebrate Abe and Reena's upcoming nuptials.

The buffet-style dinner had been catered, and Sassy had kindly offered to babysit the children of the immediate family, including Dillon, Quint's two sons and Alexa's son and daughter. So far it had been a lovely party and Leyla was looking forward to dancing in her husband's arms before the night was over.

Chuckling, Leyla patted her flat tummy. "I just had to have another dessert. You know I have a sweet tooth. Especially for a tall, dark cowboy," she added slyly.

His hand moved to splay across her stomach. "Oh, I thought you were going to tell me you were eating for two."

Carefully balancing a small plate loaded with cake in one hand, she turned to face him. "Not yet. So we'll just have to keep trying," she suggested in a low, seductive voice.

Groaning with pleasure, he bent and placed a kiss on her forehead. About that time, Quint's sister, Alexa, strolled up to them.

"Sorry to interrupt," she said. "But Quint sent me with the message that he wanted to see you two in the study."

"Both of us?" Puzzled, Leyla looked to her husband and saw a look of concern stealing across his face.

"What the hell has happened now? Thankfully, we made it without incident through mine and Leyla's reception. I was hoping we could get through this party for Abe and Reena without something bad happening."

With a placating smile, Alexa shook her head. "It's nothing like that. He has something for you. Let's go see what it is," she urged.

The study was situated on the front and western side of the house. When Laramie and Leyla entered the quiet, comfortably furnished room, Quint was already there standing behind a large, cherrywood desk. His mother, Frankie, was seated in a leather armchair. To one side of her, Abe and Reena stood with their arms wrapped around the other's waist. Maura, now heavy with child, sat across the room on a long couch, and the gaze she'd settled on Quint depicted the same eternal love Laramie felt for Leyla.

As for Quint, he was holding up a manila envelope. "Laramie, this was intended for you to receive on your wedding day with all the family present. But because Mother was feeling under the weather at that time and couldn't make it here, we had to wait until now to give it to you."

Still holding tightly to Leyla's hand, Laramie walked over to the desk. His mind was searching frantically to figure out why the whole Cantrell family was in the room.

"What is this?" Laramie asked jokingly. "An early Christmas bonus? You think I need help paying for the honeymoon that Leyla and I are going to take next month before haying season starts?"

Quint thrust the envelope at him. "I don't have a clue what's inside this thing. None of us do. For fifteen years it's been in safekeeping with a Chaparral attorney."

Dumbstruck now, Laramie glanced at the faces around him, but no one was breaking into laughs. In fact, no one was displaying any sort of amusement.

He gripped the envelope as uneasiness settled over him. "Fifteen years," Laramie said with confusion. "I was only eighteen years old then. I don't understand."

"Open the envelope, darling," Leyla urged, "and then we'll all know."

Deciding there was no point in keeping everyone waiting in suspense, Laramie tore into the manila packet. Inside was a legal-looking document consisting of several pages. Laramie didn't bother trying to decipher it. Instead, he sifted through the papers searching for a more simple explanation to the legal jargon. He found it in a single sheet of paper full of handwritten words. As he read through them, he could feel the blood draining from his face, while a strange buzzing noise sounded in his ears.

"This is incredible!" he finally managed to say as the hand holding the letter fell to his side. "I can't believe it."

"What is it?" Maura asked quickly. "You look sick!"

"Read it, Quint!" Abe instructed his grandson. "Damn it, at this rate I'll be dead before we get an answer."

"Oh, Abe, don't talk that way!" Reena scolded her fiancé. "Besides, can't you see poor Laramie is in shock? Someone get him a chair."

"I don't need a chair." With a shake of his head, Laramie handed the documents back to Quint. "This can't be possible. Look at it. Maybe I'm reading it wrong."

Quint quickly scanned the handwritten page, then gave the legal document a thorough glance. By the time he was finished, everyone in the room had gathered in a tight circle around Laramie, Leyla and Quint.

Lifting his head, Quint looked straight at Laramie and grinned. "I don't have to wonder anymore why you've always felt like my brother. You *are* my brother."

Frankie gasped and Laramie quickly turned to Lewis's widow. "I'm sorry, Frankie, I—"

Clearly annoyed with him, Quint interrupted, "Wait a minute, Laramie. You shouldn't be apologizing to Mother for something you had no control over!"

Abe shouldered his way through the bunch until he was standing directly at Laramie's side. "What does that damned letter say anyway? That Lewis fathered Laramie?"

Quint promptly handed the letter to his grandfather and Abe began to read aloud:

Dear Son, I'm writing this now because a person never knows what the future holds. And there are no guarantees I'll be around by the time you grow into a man and take a wife. If I am present on your wedding day, then clearly I've already explained the circumstances of your birth to you and this letter won't matter.

For now, you've been here on the ranch for nearly two years and with each passing day I've grown more and more proud of you. It's already clear to me that you're developing into a fine person and a good man. Diego, my old, old friend, was a wonderful father to you and I will go to my grave being ever grateful to him.

My relationship with Peggy Choney wasn't planned. She was a lonely, needy girl and I got caught up in her plight. I regret that I upended her life and betrayed my family, but I have never regretted fathering you. I can only hope that whenever the truth is finally revealed to you and the rest of the family, you will all forgive me.

God knows I should've had the courage to bring you into the family as soon as you were born. It was clear that Peggy wasn't emotionally capable of raising a baby and my dearest Frankie was, and is, such a good, loving mother. I like to think she would've taken you in her arms and called you her own. But I couldn't bring myself to take the risk of hurting her or losing you.

Deception is an awful thing, my son, and I've already lived with it far too long. On the day of your

*wedding, I want you and your wife to begin your life
with no secrets between you. Also, on this special day
I am signing over one quarter share of the Cantrell
ranch to you. I understand my gift will never com-
pensate for the mistakes that I've made, but I do hope
that the ranch will always be an important part of
you and that it will always remain your home...with
the rest of your family.*

As Abe lowered the letter, Laramie heard the sniff of
tears and realized that Leyla was one of several people in
the room wiping tears from her eyes.

"Leyla, darling," he said softly, "why are you crying?"

She gave him a brave but watery smile. "Because I'm
so happy that you finally found out about your father. And
that he loved you."

Yes, Lewis had loved him. The realization stunned
Laramie, and yet at the same time his letter made everything make sense. Diego raising him, then when he was
dying making Laramie promise to go to the Chaparral.
Lewis taking a special interest in making Laramie feel
welcome, then later teaching him all about running the
ranch. Except for Peggy Choney's whereabouts, so much
about his life had been explained

"You may not believe this, Laramie," Frankie spoke
up, "but I'm very happy, too. For a long time I've wondered and suspected that you were Lewis's son. My husband clearly had a soft spot for you. And sometimes when
I look in your eyes, I can see the same blue sparks that
were in his."

Still stunned by it all, Laramie looked to Frankie and
was amazed by the acceptance he saw on her face.

"Then you're not angry with him? Or me?"

To answer his question she stepped forward and drew

him into a tight hug. Once she released him, she said, "I had my secrets. Just like Lewis had his. But in spite of that, we loved each other very much. And how can I be angry with him? He's given me another wonderful son."

Before Laramie could make any reply to Frankie's gracious statements, Abe spoke up with a happy grin. "Hell, this ain't gonna change anything. You've been like a grandson to me for years now. This just makes it official. And now that everything is out in the open, I'm gonna have our lawyers include you in ownership of the Golden Spur Mine. That's nothin' but right. I think I can speak for everybody in the family—it's the way we all want it. The way Lewis would've wanted it."

Everyone loudly and happily agreed while Laramie shook his head with stunned amazement. "I don't know what to say."

"You don't need to say anything," Abe assured him. "We love you just as much now as we did before."

Somewhere in the group, Alexa clapped her hands together with excited glee. "I have another brother! I've got to go tell Jonas! What a time for him to go check on the kids."

She raced out of the study to find her husband, and the rest of the family continued to heap hugs and well-wishes on Laramie. He drank it all in, thinking he'd never expected that opening his heart to Leyla would also open his life to so much happiness.

Finally, Abe reminded everyone that guests were still partying out in the living room. All of them filed out of the study, but once the group started down the hall, Leyla caught Laramie by the arm to hold him back from the others.

"What is it?" he asked. "From that smile on your face, I can't imagine anything is wrong."

"I just wanted to tell you how glad I am that we didn't know about any of this before we got married."

Confused by his wife's remark, he asked, "Why would you be glad?"

"Because you're an heir. You would've thought I was marrying you for your wealth. I made such an issue of you having a place of your own and you—"

His laughter caused the rest of her words to trail away. "Oh, my precious wife," he said. "I know exactly why you married me."

"You do?" she asked slyly.

Bending his head, he brought his lips against hers. "Sure. You married me because you love me. Just as much as I love you. And like it or not, Mrs. Jones, you're part of the Cantrell family now."

Her eyes grew wide as another thought struck her. "Laramie—your name—my name. It's not really Jones. It's Cantrell. Are we going to change it?"

Unconcerned, he said, "I'll talk to the rest of the family about it. Why? Does it matter to you?"

Slipping her arms around his waist, she murmured, "Not one bit."

He was about to kiss her when from the opposite end of the long hallway, Quint shouted, "Laramie! Outside, quick! There's a fire!"

The last word sent both Laramie and Leyla flying down the hallway and through the house. Out in the backyard the family and guests had gathered to gaze at the eerie orange glow spreading across the skyline to the north of the ranch.

"Oh, God, Laramie, it looks so close!" Leyla whispered fearfully.

Grim-faced, Laramie said, "It looks like it's not far from the Pine Ridge ranch."

A few steps away, Quint was on his cell phone calling the sheriff's office in Carrizozo. At the same time one of the ranch's work trucks skidded to a halt outside the fence and Seth, the calf manager, leaped to the ground.

The tall cowboy loped up to Laramie. "Some of the hands are up there now," he said, laboring to get his breath. "They just phoned and said it looks like a hell of a fire. It's burning Chaparral and Pickens's land."

Cursing under his breath, Laramie turned to Leyla. "We'll have to go push the cattle out of there."

She nodded that she understood just as Quint ended the call and turned to Laramie.

"Brady is sending out the Forestry Division to fight the fire," Quint quickly informed him. "With everything that's been happening around here, he's already thinking arson. He's assigning Hank and Rosalinda to investigate the case."

"Good. Maybe the bastard causing all of this will finally get caught," Laramie said, then slapped his brother on the shoulder. "Let's go. We probably can't fight the fire, but we can save cattle."

"Right. I'll meet you at the horse barn."

Laramie turned back to Leyla, and the anxious expression on her face had him pulling her into the tight circle of his arms. "Leyla, darling, don't be afraid. I'll be back in no time."

Cradling his face with both hands, she gave him a brave smile. "Of course you will be. You're a Cantrell now. You have a whole new family to consider."

Dropping his head, he brought his lips close to her ear. "It's nice to be a Cantrell, Leyla. But you and Dillon are my family, my hopes and dreams. And that's the way it will always be."

She guided his mouth around to hers. "And that's the way it will always be with me, my darling."

He kissed her deeply, then hurried toward the barn to meet Quint and the rest of the cowboys.

* * * * *

Come back next month to find out what's happening on the Pine Ridge ranch in
THE DEPUTY GETS HER MAN!

REQUEST YOUR FREE BOOKS!

2 FREE NOVELS PLUS 2 FREE GIFTS!

♦ HARLEQUIN®

SPECIAL EDITION

Life, Love & Family

YES! Please send me 2 FREE Harlequin® Special Edition novels and my 2 FREE gifts (gifts are worth about $10). After receiving them, if I don't wish to receive any more books, I can return the shipping statement marked "cancel." If I don't cancel, I will receive 6 brand-new novels every month and be billed just $4.74 per book in the U.S. or $5.24 per book in Canada. That's a savings of at least 14% off the cover price! It's quite a bargain! Shipping and handling is just 50¢ per book in the U.S. and 75¢ per book in Canada.* I understand that accepting the 2 free books and gifts places me under no obligation to buy anything. I can always return a shipment and cancel at any time. Even if I never buy another book, the two free books and gifts are mine to keep forever.

235/335 HDN F45Y

Name _____ (PLEASE PRINT) _____

Address _____ Apt. # _____

City _____ State/Prov. _____ Zip/Postal Code _____

Signature (if under 18, a parent or guardian must sign) _____

Mail to the Harlequin® Reader Service:
IN U.S.A.: P.O. Box 1867, Buffalo, NY 14240-1867
IN CANADA: P.O. Box 609, Fort Erie, Ontario L2A 5X3

Want to try two free books from another line?
Call 1-800-873-8635 or visit www.ReaderService.com.

* Terms and prices subject to change without notice. Prices do not include applicable taxes. Sales tax applicable in N.Y. Canadian residents will be charged applicable taxes. Offer not valid in Quebec. This offer is limited to one order per household. Not valid for current subscribers to Harlequin Special Edition books. All orders subject to credit approval. Credit or debit balances in a customer's account(s) may be offset by any other outstanding balance owed by or to the customer. Please allow 4 to 6 weeks for delivery. Offer available while quantities last.

Your Privacy—The Harlequin® Reader Service is committed to protecting your privacy. Our Privacy Policy is available online at www.ReaderService.com or upon request from the Harlequin Reader Service.

We make a portion of our mailing list available to reputable third parties that offer products we believe may interest you. If you prefer that we not exchange your name with third parties, or if you wish to clarify or modify your communication preferences, please visit us at www.ReaderService.com/consumerchoice or write to us at Harlequin Reader Service Preference Service, P.O. Box 9062, Buffalo, NY 14269. Include your complete name and address.

HSE13R

SPECIAL EXCERPT FROM

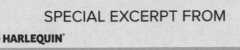

HARLEQUIN®

SPECIAL EDITION

USA TODAY *bestselling author Susan Crosby
kicks off her new Harlequin® Special Edition®
miniseries RED VALLEY RANCHERS with*
THE COWBOY'S RETURN—*a story about having
faith in love and in oneself. That's hard for single mother
Annie, even if a sexy cowboy is at her feet!*

***

"Do you have a long-range business plan?"

She laughed softly. "I love this place. I'll do anything to keep it."

"There's no sense driving yourself to an early grave over a piece of land, Annie."

"Spoken like a vagabond. Well, I've been a vagabond. Roots are so much better." She shoved away from the railing. "I have work to do."

Annie went inside, her good mood having fizzled. What did he know about the need to own, to succeed? He didn't have a child to support and raise right. Who was he to give such advice?

Mitch hadn't come in by the time Austin went to bed and she'd showered and retreated to her own room. It wasn't even dark yet. She pulled down her shades, blocking the dusky sky. Usually she dropped off almost the instant her head hit the pillow.

Tonight she listened for sounds of him, the stranger she was trusting to treat her and her son right. After a while, she heard him come in, then the click of the front door lock.

A few minutes later the shower came on. She pictured him shampooing his hair, which curled down his neck a little, inviting fingers to twine it gently.

Some time passed after the water turned off. Was he shaving? Yes. She could hear the tap of his razor against the sink edge. If they were a couple, he would be coming to bed clean and smooth shaven….

The bathroom door opened and closed, followed by his bedroom door. After that there was only the quiet of a country night, marked occasionally by an animal rustling beyond her open window. She'd finally stopped jumping at strange noises, had stopped getting up to look out her window, wondering what was there. She could identify most of the sounds now.

And tonight she would sleep even better, knowing a strong man was next door. She could give up her fears for a while, get a solid night's sleep and face the new day not alone, not putting on a show of being okay and in control for Austin.

Now if she could just do something about her suddenly-come-to-life libido, all would be right in her world.

***

Don't miss **A COWBOY'S RETURN** *by USA TODAY bestselling author Susan Crosby.*

Available June 2013 from Harlequin® Special Edition® wherever books are sold.

Love the Harlequin book you just read?

Your opinion matters.

Review this book on your favorite book site, review site, blog or your own social media properties and share your opinion with other readers!